DANE

DANE

TEXAS BOUDREAU BROTHERHOOD

By
KATHY IVAN

COPYRIGHT

DANE – Texas Boudreau Brotherhood Book #10

Dane Boudreau's hidden a secret his entire life. Somebody wants to make sure that secret gets buried—along with Dane—permanently. Hacker Destiny Smith discovers a contract on Dane's life and offers to track down the person gunning for him. Between a quickie elopement to Vegas and dangers lurking closer to home, Dane and Destiny must figure out who wants him six feet under before that wish becomes a reality and ends their chance at happiness.

"In Shiloh Springs, Kathy Ivan has crafted warm, engaging characters that will steal your heart and a mystery that will keep you reading to the very last page." Barb Han, USA TODAY and Publisher's Weekly Bestselling Author

Kathy Ivan's books are addictive, you can't read just one." Susan Stoker, NYT Bestselling Author

BOOKS BY KATHY IVAN

www.kathyivan.com/books.html

TEXAS BOUDREAU BROTHERHOOD

Rafe

Antonio

Brody

Ridge

Lucas

Heath

Shiloh

Chance

Derrick

Dane

Liam (coming soon)

Brian (coming soon)

NEW ORLEANS CONNECTION SERIES

Desperate Choices

Connor's Gamble

Relentless Pursuit

Ultimate Betrayal

Keeping Secrets

Sex, Lies and Apple Pies

Deadly Justice

Wicked Obsession

Hidden Agenda

Spies Like Us

Fatal Intentions

New Orleans Connection Series Box Set: Books 1-3

New Orleans Connection Series Box Set: Books 4-7

Hello Readers,

Welcome to Shiloh Springs, Texas! Don't you just love a small Texas town where the people are neighborly, the gossip plentiful, and the heroes are...well, heroic, not to mention easy on the eyes! I love everything about Texas, which I why I've made the great state my home for over thirty years. There's no other place like it. From the delicious Tex-Mex food and downhome barbecue, the majestic scenery and friendly atmosphere, the people and places of the Lone Star state are as unique and colorful as you'll find anywhere.

The Texas Boudreau Brotherhood series centers on a group of foster brothers, men who would have ended up in the system if not for Douglas and Patricia Boudreau. Instead of being hardened by life's hardships and bad circumstances beyond their control, they found a family who loved and accepted them, and gave them a place to call home. Sometimes brotherhood is more than sharing the same DNA.

While there are a lot of Boudreau brothers (and we can't forget their sister, Nica), there are also some interesting characters that have made their way into Shiloh Springs and into readers hearts, and I know you're curious about some of them. So, I'm going to be writing stories about some of them, like Brian. Brian showed up in Chance's book and now he's making an appearance in Dane's book too. He's an interesting man with a sketchy past, so I think he's going to be fun to write. And he loves Ms. Patti, so he can't be all bad, can he?

Dane's been hiding secrets from his family for a long time, and now those secrets are about to explode. And when

Destiny Smith, hacker extraordinaire, shows up telling him somebody's put a contract on his life, things really get interesting. Between a quickie elopement to Vegas to danger lurking closer to home, Dane and Destiny must figure out who wants Dane six feet under before that wish becomes a reality and ends their chance at happiness.

If you've read my other romantic suspense books (the New Orleans Connection series and Cajun Connection series), you'll be familiar with the Boudreau name. Turns out there are a whole lot of Boudreaus out there, just itching to have their stories told. (Douglas is the brother of Gator Boudreau, patriarch of the New Orleans branch of the Boudreau family. The New Orleans Boudreaus have their stories told in the New Orleans Connection Series.) Oh, and did I mention Gator and Douglas have another brother – Hank "The Tank" Boudreau? I see another series of Boudreaus in my writing future.)

So, sit back and relax. The pace of small-living might be less hectic than the big city, but small towns hold secrets, excitement, and heroes who ride to the rescue. And don't you just love a Texas cowboy?

Kathy Ivan

EDITORIAL REVIEWS

"In Shiloh Springs, Kathy Ivan has crafted warm, engaging characters that will steal your heart and a mystery that will keep you reading to the very last page."

—Barb Han, *USA TODAY* and Publisher's Weekly Bestselling Author

"Kathy Ivan's books are addictive, you can't read just one."

—Susan Stoker, NYT Bestselling Author

"Kathy Ivan's books give you everything you're looking for and so much more."

—Geri Foster, USA Today and NYT Bestselling Author of the Falcon Securities Series

"This is the first I have read from Kathy Ivan and it won't be the last."

—Night Owl Reviews

"I highly recommend Desperate Choices. Readers can't go wrong here!"

—Melissa, Joyfully Reviewed

"I loved how the author wove a very intricate storyline with plenty of intriguing details that led to the final reveal..."

—Night Owl Reviews

Desperate Choices—Winner 2012 International Digital Award—Suspense

Desperate Choices—Best of Romance 2011 –Joyfully Reviewed

DEDICATIONS AND ACKNOWLEDGEMENTS

To my readers—those who've been with me since the beginning, and those who've just joined me on my journey, YOU are the reason I keep writing. Knowing the Boudreau family touches your hearts and lives makes me so happy, and makes me want to writer faster, so I can give you the next brothers' story.

To my sister, Mary. She knows why.

As always, I dedicate this and every book to my mother, Betty Sullivan. Her love of reading introduced me to books at a young age. I will always cherish the memories of talking books and romance with her. I know she's looking down on me and smiling.

More about Kathy and her books can be found at

WEBSITE:
www.kathyivan.com

Follow Kathy on Facebook at
facebook.com/kathyivanauthor

Follow Kathy on Twitter at
twitter.com/@kathyivan

Follow Kathy at BookBub
bookbub.com/profile/kathy-ivan

NEWSLETTER SIGN UP

Don't want to miss out on any new books, contests, and free stuff? Sign up to get my newsletter. I promise not to spam you, and only send out notifications/e-mails whenever there's a new release or contest/giveaway. Follow the link and join today!

http://eepurl.com/baqdRX

DANE

CHAPTER ONE

S OMEBODY WANTS ME *dead.*

Pulling into Juanita's parking lot, Dane Boudreau cut the engine in his pickup, his gaze scanning the busy Tex-Mex restaurant's entrance. He'd told Destiny Smith he'd meet her here. How could he not, after her cryptic phone call? Finding out somebody's put a hit on your life wasn't something he heard every day, and hopefully, Ridge's pet hacker would be able to provide more details. Maybe a who, what, or why.

Like I don't already know why. This day has been coming for a long time.

Spotting the pretty dark-haired pixie pacing back and forth by the restaurant's front doors had him smiling. From what little he'd seen and heard about the gamine beauty; she was a stick of dynamite contained in a petite package. Ridge bragged about her skills with a computer, and Dane wondered how she harnessed all that vitality long enough to sit in front of a monitor.

She spotted him before he got halfway across the parking lot, and he watched her sigh. Yeah, she definitely appeared frazzled, though the look of relief that crossed her face confused him. Destiny barely knew him; he was little more than a stranger she might pass on the street. So why the concern for his safety?

"Sorry I had to pull you from your family get-together, but I didn't think this could wait."

"I got that impression from your call." Dane reached past Destiny's shoulder and pulled open Juanita's front door, motioning for her to precede him. "Let's grab a table, and you can tell me all about what you've uncovered."

Destiny shot him a glare, which might have a lesser man cringing, and Dane winced under her disapproval. Right, he needed to dial back his sarcasm. She hadn't done anything wrong, per se. Keeping an eye out for his family was a good thing, he reminded himself.

They didn't speak again until they'd been led to a table, and seated, and given their drink orders to the friendly waitress. Dane watched her run a hand across her face, noting the dark circles beneath her eyes. While she still vibrated with tension, it was obvious she hadn't been getting a lot of sleep. Somehow, the idea of her tossing and turning throughout a sleepless night disturbed him on a deep level.

"You dropped your bombshell and hung up before I could ask any questions." Dane leaned against the padded back of the booth and crossed his arms over his chest. "Care to give me a few more details?"

Destiny stared down at her hands, twining her fingers

over and over. All that nervous energy needed to go someplace. Dane had the feeling she wasn't one to sit idly. It was almost like she wanted—no, needed—to be working a keyboard rather than sitting here. Unfortunately, this wasn't a social meeting where he could simply let her off the hook and send her on her way. No, the information she'd uncovered might make the difference in his investigation. One nobody, especially his family, knew anything about. And he planned to keep it that way.

This is personal.

"Like I said, I like Ridge. He's a decent boss and lets me do my job on my terms. He told me a little about his past, how he ended up a Boudreau. Talked about your family and how much you all mean to him. So, I kind of keep my eyes open whenever I see the Boudreau name pop up online. Thank goodness you don't spell your last name like the Louisiana Boudreauxs. Having that X on the end really skews the results."

"From what I understand, generations ago our family spelled it with the X on the end. I have no idea when it changed, but…"

He stopped talking as Destiny huffed out a breath, and it ruffled the bangs across her forehead in a cute way. Most of the time he loved long hair on women, something he never questioned. It just was. But Destiny's shorter hair, feathered in spiky layers around her face, and highlighted her high cheekbones and made her eyes seem huge.

"I set up a few alerts so any time one of your names' popped up, from anybody doing any type of inquiry, from a casual search to a credit check, I get notified. Ninety-nine percent of the time it's nothing. Almost everybody who's on the internet has tons of stuff moving through various sites and they never know about it. Usually, they're simple surface inquiries. Like when somebody looks up Camilla, because of her books. Things like that I discard without a second glance. Ms. Patti's real estate business? Douglas' construction company? Tons of hits but nothing that would raise any red flags."

"But something about my name did?"

She nodded, nibbling on her lower lip. Dane fisted his hands to keep from reaching across the table and touching her lip, to pull it free. He didn't understand why he reacted to Destiny like this. Ever since he'd seen her in the Big House's kitchen with Tina, saw the colorful tattoo above her breast, he couldn't stop thinking about her. And that was a problem. Until he'd settled all the issues with his own life, he couldn't even think about dealing with anything or anybody else.

"How much do you know about the internet?"

Dane barely refrained from rolling his eyes at Destiny's abrupt change of topic. While he wasn't a complete noob, he had more than a passing knowledge of the ins and outs of the World Wide Web. Not as much as Destiny, obviously, but still…

"I get by."

"There is the internet, the general websites, where everyone does their daily business. Whenever you do any kind of search, that's where you're looking. But there is a deeper layer called the Dark Web. That's where a lot of your more…questionable…searches and requests happen."

Dane nodded, following her meaning. "I've heard of the Dark Web. That's where you found my name?"

"Yeah. At first, I thought it was a mistake. That happens sometimes. Some idiot types in a wrong URL and gets steered to a place where they'd never really go, and usually gets redirected pretty quick."

Destiny stopped talking when their server brought their drinks, along with chips, salsa, and queso. Dane tapped the corner of the menu, and she shook her head, choosing instead to grab a tortilla chip, and scoop up a mound of queso and pop it into her mouth. A smile curved upward at the look of total bliss on her face. Well, that answered one question. The woman liked Mexican food. He wondered what else might put that look on her face, and immediately vetoed that train of thought. He didn't have time to get involved with a woman—especially one who worked for his brother.

"Let's cut to the chase, Destiny. You got an alert with my name. Found somebody ordered a hit on me. What else do you have? A time? A place? A name? Give me something."

Her intense perusal made him feel like a bug under a

microscope. She didn't say a word, simply studied him with such ferocity he wanted to do something. Anything. Mostly he wanted to bolt from the restaurant, pretend he'd never heard about somebody wanting him dead. Unfortunately, that wasn't an option. He'd managed to stay hidden from the rest of the world, the people who'd been looking for him for most of his life. Living with the Boudreaus, being adopted at an early age, and changing his name had helped keep his pursuers off his trail for almost two decades.

But, if they had *this* name, the Boudreau connection, it meant they'd found him. And that changed everything.

DESTINY KEPT HER head lowered and shoved another queso-loaded chip into her mouth. Maybe if she kept shoving food in her face, he wouldn't notice how nervous she was. While most people didn't intimidate or frighten her, Dane Boudreau was the exception. All the fear bundled deep inside had nothing to do with thinking he would physically hurt her. Just the opposite. The man fascinated her to the point of obsession. And she was afraid that obsession, looking and digging to find out more about the enigmatic man who occupied her thoughts during the day and her dreams at night, had triggered something online and brought all kinds of unwanted attention down on his head. If this turned out to be her fault, she'd never forgive herself.

"Destiny?" Fingers snapped in front of her face, and she blinked, realizing she'd zoned out. In front of Dane Boudreau. *What an idiot!* Heat spread across her cheeks, and she brushed her hands against her jean-clad thighs, trying to wick away all the sweat on her palms. Sheesh, she was acting like this was a first date and she was a teenager in junior high school with a crush on the captain of the football team.

"Sorry. Yeah, it was buried deep on a site used by mercenaries. Not the wannabe, magazine-loving soldier of fortune geeks who think being macho means carrying around an AK-47 deep in the woods and taking selfies makes them all manly. No, this was a legitimate site, authentic with real hired killers. And a post with a significant bounty on *your head.*"

Grabbing her margarita, she took a big swallow, choking at the strong alcohol taste. Dane's lips curved into a smile, and he lifted his beer in salute.

Good grief, can I embarrass myself any more in front of him?

"How much?" Dane threw the question out, his tone casual. From his slouched posture and nonchalant attitude, she could almost believe they were talking about something innocuous, like the weather. Not discussing the fact somebody wanted him dead. Like a bullet between the eyes, cold as a kipper on a cracker, dead.

"What?"

"How much is somebody willing to pay to see me six feet

under?"

Destiny closed her eyes and counted to five, because the urge to wrap her hands around his neck and squeeze was overwhelming. Did the man never take anything seriously? Or was this his default position when threatened? Too bad she didn't know him well enough to tell if sarcasm was his normal default mode when confronted.

"Two hundred?"

He chuckled. "They're only willing to pay two hundred dollars to have me bumped off?"

"Dane, will you take this seriously? Not two hundred dollars. *Two hundred thousand dollars.* Definitely not chump change. Somebody has a real hankering to see you die. Want to tell me why?"

"How would I know?"

Destiny's eyes narrowed at his flippant response. From his carefully blank expression, she knew he was hiding something. He might be good at hiding his feelings, but she was an expert at assessing bull hockey, and he was full of it up to his eyeballs. Nothing added up, and the itch between her shoulder blades told her he knew exactly why somebody wanted him six feet under. Not that she had any intention of letting anybody get close enough to take a pot shot at Dane Boudreau.

"Dane, you don't know me well, so I'll be upfront about my intentions. You're not taking my warning seriously, which makes me suspicious you know more than you're letting on. It's almost as if—no, tell me you didn't already know about—son of a gun, you did!"

Dane picked at the edge of the label on his beer, refusing to meet her gaze, and she knew she was right. *What a jerk!* He'd left her spinning in the wind, trying to make heads or tails of the purported death threat, and he already knew somebody was after him.

"I didn't know." He held up a hand when she started to interrupt. "Let's just say I've been anticipating it happening most of my life." He pointed at her, his steely-eyed stare boring into her. "You cannot tell anybody. Not Ridge, none of my family. Especially Momma and Dad. I'll take care of the problem, and they never have to know."

Her head spun, a plethora of possibilities racing through her brain. Why wouldn't he want his family to know? They'd help him, of that she had not a single doubt. She'd heard enough about Ms. Patti to know if there was a threat to any of her kids, she'd circle the wagons like they'd done in the Wild West, and have so much protection around them, nobody could get close enough to touch one of her babies. Yet Dane refused his family's assistance and support.

"Why?"

"It's too dangerous. I'm not dragging anybody into a situation that could put them at risk. I've been waiting over twenty years for this threat to appear, and I'll take care of it. My family doesn't need to get involved."

Twenty years? He'd been anticipating somebody trying to

kill him for twenty years! No way I'm walking away without knowing why…and what I can do to thwart their plans.

"I'm already involved, you can't shut me out. Or shut me up for that matter." Destiny crossed her arms over her chest and shot him a smug look.

"Wanna bet?"

"Sure. You seem to forget, Mr. Boudreau, I don't work for you. You have no control over me financially or otherwise. You cannot, as my niece would say, tell me what to do. If I want to go to your brother with this information, there is nothing to stop me. I can simply say I found it as part of my daily work and bring it to his attention. Same with your mom and dad. They won't care how I came across the information, but I know darn good and well they'll act on it. You'll find yourself hogtied and wrapped in cotton wool so fast you won't know what hit you."

"You wouldn't."

Destiny allowed a slow smile to cross her lips and tried to keep her satisfaction out of her voice. "Your choice. You can tell me who's after you and we can come up with a game plan to thwart the hired gun, or…" She let her words trail off, the implication clear.

Gotcha.

Dane rubbed a hand over his face, and Destiny knew she had him. The suspense was driving her nuts, because she'd tried to dig into who'd placed the ad for the hit, but so far all she'd found were rabbit trails. Somebody had buried the information good and deep, but they'd never be able to bury it deep enough. She had programs running right now at her apartment, computer searches digging into each rerouting of the signal, digging through each dummy corporation and brick wall. Somebody had a good IT guy working for them—but she was better. And she never gave up on solving a puzzle.

Dane sighed and plunked his beer bottle down on the table in front of him. "I want your word. Nothing I tell you or show you goes beyond us. I repeat—nobody finds out. Not Ridge, not my brothers. *Especially not my parents.*"

She almost winced at the edge in his voice when he mentioned his parents. For the briefest moment, she hesitated, because what he was asking was big. Destiny didn't give a promise lightly. Too many times in the past she'd been burned by people making and breaking their pledges, so once she committed to something, she stayed the course to the end. Finally, she held out her hand, and found it swallowed within his callus-roughened one.

"I promise."

Dane grabbed his beer bottle and tipped it back, draining it in a long swallow. He pointed to her glass. "Finish up and let's go."

"Where?"

"The ranch. Specifically, the foreman's house where I live. I've got to show you something."

Destiny gulped the remnants of her margarita and stood

pulling her keys from her jeans pocket. Tilting her brow, she taunted him.

"What are we waiting for? Let's go."

CHAPTER TWO

D ANE PULLED HIS pickup in front of the two-story foreman's house and killed the engine. The headlights illuminated the front porch with its square columns and the porch swing on the left-hand side. The white paint had faded some with age since it hadn't been painted in a few years. He'd moved into the foreman's house five years earlier when he'd taken over the responsibility for the Boudreau ranch. With the long hours, and getting up before dawn most mornings, it only made sense. Especially when each of his brothers decided to pursue jobs that kept them away from the ranch. Sure, they helped out whenever they could, since they all loved the ranch and the entire spread that belonged to the family, but not like he did. The land grounded him in a way he couldn't explain. It gave him the roots he'd craved growing up.

His feelings had nothing to do with feeling unloved, just the opposite. Momma and Dad made sure he knew he was wanted. Loved. That he belonged in a family where every single one of them knew they'd been chosen. Cherished. Yet the land spoke to him, gave him a purpose. Raising the cattle, through sickness and crazy weather, vet visits, and the occasional rustler gave him a feeling of accomplishment a nine-to-five job never could. He knew because he'd tried that route. It had been an unmitigated failure.

A single headlight appeared behind him, followed by the growling rumble of a motorcycle, which pulled up beside his truck with a barely controlled roar. The feminine curves straddling the big beast didn't surprise him. He noted the leather pants on Destiny earlier and had watched her pull on a weather-beaten leather jacket before he'd pulled out of Juanita's parking lot.

Destiny alighted from the motorcycle and strode forward, confidence guiding every step. Stopping beside the pickup's driver's open window, she propped an elbow in the opening and shot him a cocky grin.

"You gonna sit here all night, cowboy, or are we going inside? I can't wait to see what you've got to show me." Giving him a flirty wink, she sauntered toward the front porch, lightly climbing the steps to stand beside the front door. Silently chuckling, he couldn't help thinking she looked as good walking away as she did coming.

Breathing deeply, he paused on the first porch step, inhaling the scent of the night-blooming jasmine that climbed along the columns on the right side of the porch, its sweet fragrance perfuming the darkness. He loved sleeping with his windows open, letting the familiar flowers' smell lull him to sleep.

Opening the front door, he watched Destiny, gauging her reaction to his home. Why, he wasn't sure, but there was a deep-seated desire for her to like the place. And that was crazy. Her opinion shouldn't matter one way or the other—yet it did.

The old farmhouse wasn't modernized, except for the kitchen. He'd preferred leaving the homey touches the way it had been when the original Boudreaus lived here before the Big House had been built. A sense of history oozed from each floorboard, every nook and cranny revealing its own story. While he loved the Big House and its sense of family, to him the original farmhouse was home.

"This place is amazing. Look at that molding. And the staircase. It's original, isn't it?"

"Yes. This is the old house. Dad's grandparents built it when they bought the property, so it's been around for a long time. Mostly it was the foreman's house, but now it's mine."

"It's awesome. The character. The history. I bet if these walls could talk, they'd have some interesting stories to tell." She spun in a slow circle, her arms outstretched. "I love older homes. The sense that people cherished them, loved and cared for them, it's ingrained with each nail. Every scuff and scrape. You're lucky to have a place with these kinds of memories."

Dane swallowed at the look of undisguised longing on her face as Destiny ran her hand along the banister. Every word she'd said rang with the truth. Looking at her, with her short hair and tattoos, riding a motorcycle that seemed almost too big for her to handle, he'd expected her to be all about modern touches. Chrome and glass. Sharp angles and minimalism. Guess he had to revise his opinion. Little Miss Destiny was full of surprises.

"Can I get you anything? Something to drink?"

She shook her head. "I'm good."

He shoved his hands into the back pockets of his jeans, wondering not for the first time that night if he'd made a mistake bringing her here. Sure, she'd discovered the link on the mercenary site, with the alleged hit on him. That didn't mean he should share his info with her. But something inside, some gut instinct—one he didn't want to ignore—told him it would be worth it. He believed her when she'd given her word not to tell anyone. When the time was right, he planned on explaining everything to his family. They deserved the truth, but he wasn't ready. Because they'd be hurt, which was the last thing he wanted.

"Come on, Dane, quit stalling. You said you had some-thing to show me, something which would make the threat on your life make sense. Spill it, cowboy."

"What's your hurry?"

She rolled her eyes. "Have you glanced at a clock recent-ly? It's late. I'm tired, and I still have work to get done when I get home." She shot him a look, her mouth turning down in a frown. "Please tell me you didn't bring me here on some wild goose chase, trying to convince me not to keep digging. If that's your plan, it ain't gonna happen."

Dane sighed, knowing he couldn't put it off any longer. Besides, Destiny was smart. Maybe she'd notice something he'd missed.

"Follow me, princess."

"Princess?" She gave an inelegant snort. "Boy, have you got the wrong idea, cowboy. Nobody could be further from a princess than me."

"You call me cowboy."

"Well, you deal with cows and you're a guy, so…"

"Touché." He gestured toward the stairs. "Follow me."

They climbed the stairs to the second floor, and he led her to a door at the end of the hallway, which opened to another set of steps. Climbing them, he made his way into the attic. His hand reached for the switch beside the door, and bright overhead lights illuminated the whole area. The unvarnished floorboards, weathered and gray with age, ran the length of the space. Stacks of cardboard boxes lined the far wall, each painstakingly labeled in bold black print. Things from each generation of Boudreaus who'd resided here before him, cherished mementos, sentimental items nobody could bring themselves to get rid of. He strode past them without stopping. Past the old trunk that had belonged to his father's mother. Past the Christmas decorations packaged with care, stacked neatly to avoid damage.

Destiny's footsteps had stopped at the top of the stairs,

before tentatively moving forward. When he turned, he caught her running a gentle hand over a stack of quilts sitting atop the weathered seat of an old rocking chair, one that used to sit on the front porch. At her soft touch, almost a caress, his breath caught in the back of his throat. She was full of surprises, and he fought back the urge to discover each one. Not now, maybe not ever. He couldn't afford to lose focus on his goal, the one driving him.

"Over here."

Her gaze shifted to meet his at his words, and she shrugged, a chagrined expression on her face. "Sorry. I tend to get distracted in places like this. There's so much to see and explore." Brushing her hands against her thighs, she added, "Okay, I'm done. What's that?" She pointed toward the huge stand behind him, draped with an old sheet.

Without a word, he whipped it off, twirling it like a magician revealing his latest trick. Set on an easel, the large whiteboard was double-sided like a classroom chalkboard, and he'd covered just about every inch of space on both sides. His research from the last few years, notes of everything he remembered from his childhood, filled columns. Each one was headed with a name, handwritten facts, figures, and any information he'd gleaned during his investigation.

Destiny moved to stand at his side, her eyes studying all the information, the rumors, and innuendos. He'd left nothing off.

"Thorough. What exactly am I looking at?"

"The story of my life." He tossed out the answer like a live grenade and waited for the inevitable explosion.

"What a load of…" Destiny's words broke off and her fist landing against his upper arm stung. She hadn't pulled her punch, and he resisted the urge to rub at the offending area.

"Let me finish, princess. This," he waved his hand toward the whiteboard, "is the story of everything I remember about my life before coming to live with Douglas and Ms. Patti."

"Oh." She gave him a chagrined half-smile, shrugging like that would make up for the fact she'd smashed her fist into his arm. "Sorry. It's just a lot to take in; especially considering some of the names you've got written there."

"I've been compiling this information for a long time. Everything you're seeing is true. Names, dates, places. The big question is—which one of them hates me enough to want me dead?"

"You believe me about the hit? I thought maybe you were simply humoring me because I work for Shiloh and Ridge."

Dane studied Destiny's face, read her genuine concern. He'd expected skepticism or downright cynicism to his findings, but all he felt from her was an undertone of warmth and acceptance he'd hardly anticipated. He'd half expected her to take one look at his findings and walk straight back out the door.

"With everything I've discovered, I'm honestly surprised one of them hasn't come after me sooner. The only saving grace I have is they didn't know where I lived or my name until recently. Dane Boudreau is my legal name, but it isn't the one I was born with. When I went into the foster care system, the only information they had for me was a letter and this." Reaching beneath his shirt, he pulled out the thin gold chain with the small medallion hanging from it.

"May I see it?"

Pulling the chain over his head, he handed it to Destiny and saw her eyes widen when she recognized the symbol engraved on one side. Her fingertip traced the image, and he swore he felt her fingers touch it like she ran them along his skin. A shudder racked his body, and he pulled himself free of the image in his brain. He wasn't surprised when her eyes widened as she flipped the medallion over, and she read the words.

"This is—are you sure?" The words were barely above a whisper, husky and tinged with an eerie sense of acceptance. "Dude, if this gets out, every news agency in the U.S. will be on your doorstep. Heck, probably most of the free world press. I mean, seriously, this is big. Bigger than big. Holy amazeballs, Dane."

"It's true. I hadn't planned to do or say anything to any-body, not until I had enough documentation to bring to the authorities. Unfortunately, I think one of my searches must have triggered a failsafe or something, because about six months ago things on the web started disappearing. Records I'd downloaded vanished, like they'd never existed. Fortunately, I backed everything up onto a computer that isn't connected to the internet, or whoever it is might have been able to hack in and get rid of everything."

Destiny started pacing as he talked, her footsteps measured and precise. Eight steps in one direction, turn, eight steps back. He could practically hear the wheels turning inside her head, working out each step he'd taken to find and secure the facts he'd been able to compile.

"You've obviously pissed off somebody. Probably one of the people you've listed there," she gestured toward the whiteboard. "Dane, you know these are dangerous people, right? Every single one of them has money and power. They won't be happy to discover somebody who will upset their applecart. That's what you're planning, right?"

Dane watched Destiny clench the medallion in her closed fist, and gently peeled back her fingers, pulling the chain free. He stared at the gold, its shine worn with age. A memory of a lovely woman with smiling eyes wearing the necklace popped into his mind, remembered her pulling it over her head and placing it around his neck. The chain hung low on his childish frame, but he'd grinned like he'd been given the best prize in the world.

"Promise me you'll take good care of this until I come home." Her voice, warm and soothing as honey, teased at his senses. A wave of sorrow threatened, and he quashed it down.

"I promise, Mommy."

"You are my little man. So brave and strong. Daddy and I will be home before you know it. Be good for Ginger." She leaned forward and whispered, "She promised ice cream after supper, but don't let her know I told you. It's supposed to be a surprise."

Wrapping his arms around her neck, he squeezed her close, felt the tears pricking behind his eyelids. He didn't want her to go. Wanted to beg her to stay with him. But he didn't, because her and Daddy had to go and do business. He wasn't sure what business was, but he hated it. "I promise, Mommy."

"Dane?"

Destiny's voice yanked him from the memory, fading away like an ephemeral cloud. He hadn't thought about that night for years. Time had dulled the knife-edge of pain, but not the rage that burned, vivid and all-consuming, within him.

"Sorry, I got lost in thought for a second."

Destiny walked over to the easel and tapped it with her finger. "All this—do Douglas and Ms. Patti know?"

Ah, there was the question he'd been expecting, ever since he'd brought her into the attic. Because he knew she wasn't going to like his answer.

"No. And you can't tell them."

CHAPTER THREE

DESTINY WIPED HER hands against the skirt of her sundress, wondering again if she'd lost her ever-loving mind. She must have, because she was wearing a dress—*a dress for criminy sake*—and she was sitting in a pew in the middle of a church service in Shiloh Springs. The last time she'd been inside a church was so long ago she barely remembered it. Yet here she was, bright and early on a Sunday morning, listening to the choir sing and praying she didn't fall asleep halfway through the service.

She hadn't slept a wink after she left Dane's place the night before, her mind whirling with all the information she'd garnered. It felt surreal, almost like a dream, because the information he'd shared was too farfetched to be true. He couldn't have surprised her more if he'd lobbed a live grenade into her hands like a hot potato. Yet the facts he'd presented, the data and painstaking research he had done, all led to the same conclusion. An unsolved secret over two decades old. A secret so potentially life-changing, somebody wanted it to stay dead and buried.

Of course, Dane's revelation explained the huge bounty

on his head. Seemed the idiot thought he was invincible. Ten feet tall and bulletproof. The knot in her stomach, the one that'd been there all night, tightened as she pictured him lying in a casket at the front of this church. Balling her hands into fists, nails digging into her palms, she drew in a ragged breath and swore she wasn't going to let that happen. It would break something inside her to see him pale and lifeless. Not Dane. He was a vibrant, shining light. One she wanted to delve into, bask in its warmth.

She stood when everyone else did, heard the preacher give the final prayer to dismiss the service, and realized she'd missed the whole thing, so caught up in her thoughts to hear a single word.

"Destiny?"

She glanced in the direction of the masculine voice, recognizing it immediately. She gave a rueful smile. "Good morning, boss."

Shiloh shot her a curious look, his arm wrapped around his fiancée, Mary Margaret White, lovingly referred to as Maggie. She couldn't get over how happy he was now that he'd met the love of his life. While working on a case, he'd fallen hard for the woman he was investigating, and helped the DEA catch the real drug smugglers who were using Maggie's land to funnel drugs through Texas.

"Are you heading over to the Big House for lunch?"

"No. I haven't been to church in a while and felt the need for a little divine guidance."

Oops, I probably shouldn't have said that. Now he's gonna want to know what's wrong.

"Anything I can help with?" Shiloh's immediate offer of help didn't surprise Destiny. All the Boudreaus she'd met were like that. They were the first ones to step up in a crisis and offer help, and they held their friends in the highest regard. She'd felt an immediate kinship with Shiloh from their first interview, and she hadn't hesitated to take him up on his job offer, though she'd originally started out working for his brother, Ridge. Though she could have worked remotely and stayed in California, she'd loaded everything she owned into a rental truck and headed for Texas without a qualm in the world. Of course, it wasn't hard when you don't have roots tying you to any one place, she mused.

"It's nothing, I promise."

"Well, if you're not busy, why don't you join us for lunch? Dad's firing up the grill, and we're all heading up to the Big House." Shiloh issued the invitation with a smile.

"Destiny? It's lovely to see you here this morning."

Uh-oh. Busted by Momma Boudreau.

"Good morning, Ms. Patti. It's nice to see you, too."

Patti Boudreau wore a pretty shirtwaist dress in a soft blush pink with buttons down the front and matching pumps. Her blond hair was styled in the way Destiny was used to seeing her, teased and backcombed to give it additional volume and added height. Being a petite woman, Ms. Patti always remarked she needed the additional inches to be visible in the sea of Boudreau menfolk, all of whom topped six feet. Destiny doubted anybody with half a brain would be able to overlook or ignore Patti Boudreau. The woman was a ball of energy and determination, with a personality that could dominate any crowd or situation.

"I heard Shiloh invite you to lunch. Please come. We haven't had a chance to really get to know each other, though you've worked for this one," she jerked a thumb at Shiloh, "for months now. Besides, we could use a few more women around today. I'm outnumbered and drowning in testosterone, especially with Nica back at school."

"I appreciate the offer, but I've got some work I—"

Before she could finish her sentence, Ms. Patti rounded on Shiloh. "You're working her too hard. Sunday's supposed to be a day of rest, son. I thought your daddy and I taught you better."

Shiloh raised both hands. "Whoa, don't blame me." He shot Destiny a side-eye glare. "As far as I know, she finished what she was working on. I haven't even had a chance to talk to her about the new assignment—which I was going to do in the morning." His half-accusatory tone made Destiny wince. It hadn't been her intention to get her boss in trouble with his mother. Plus, now he was going to start snooping into what she was working on outside her regular work. And she couldn't afford to have Shiloh start digging. Not after she'd given her word to Dane not to say anything to his family.

"Ms. Patti, when I said work, I didn't mean job-related stuff. It's simply a side project I'm doing in my spare time. More of a hobby you might say."

A satisfied smirk tugged at Ms. Patti's lips. "Then I guess that means you can come for lunch. We'll expect you at the ranch." When she motioned Shiloh closer with a crooked finger, he leaned in, and she brushed a kiss against his cheek. Destiny's gaze caught Maggie's, who rolled her eyes and grinned. Guess she was used to the way the Boudreaus got what they wanted.

After Ms. Patti walked past, followed by Douglas, Destiny grabbed the small bag she'd shoved her wallet and keys into that morning. It felt odd carrying such a tiny purse when she was used to hauling everything around in a backpack. She'd figured, rightly, the camouflaged patterned backpack wouldn't jibe with her church clothes, and she'd been right.

"You need a lift to the Big House?" Shiloh's hand lightly touched her arm. She'd almost forgotten he stood there with his fiancée because her mind was already wondering how long she'd have to stay for lunch before she could find an excuse to get back to her computer and dig for more. Information was her lifeblood, the thrill and excitement of digging and uncovering long-hidden and ofttimes forgotten tidbits was like an adrenaline-high to a junkie.

"Thanks, but I've got my car."

"Great. See you there." He and Maggie walked past her,

and she followed behind them, passing Lucas and Jill on her way to the door. Spotting Heath and Camilla, she gave them a brief wave and shuffled out as quickly as she could, finally taking a deep breath once she slid behind the wheel of her nondescript sedan. Closing her eyes, she leaned her head against the steering wheel. A sharp rap on the passenger-side window had her jerking upright, and she stared into the eyes of Dane Boudreau. He motioned for her to lower the window.

"Momma said you're coming to the Big House for lunch. Mind giving me a ride? It'll give us a chance to talk."

Giving him a brief nod, she waited until he climbed in and put on his seatbelt, then headed for Main Street. She didn't say a word, deciding it would be prudent to let him initiate their talk. After all, the drive to the Boudreau ranch wasn't a quick one. The sprawling estate—because she really couldn't call it anything else—was nearly an hour outside Shiloh Springs. At least the official township. The whole thing was part of Shiloh Springs County and had been for generations. The Boudreaus had been part of the founding families of the town, something she had a tough time wrapping her head around. She'd never landed in one place long enough to call it home, much less had the kind of generational history they claimed.

"Sorry I dumped all my mess on you last night." Dane's deep voice held a hint of the Texas twang she associated with all the Boudreau guys. Each one of them epitomized the All-

American cowboy, from the way they dressed to the way they talked. It wasn't the stylized kind of metrosexual cowboy persona depicted by Hollywood in the movies. Nope, these guys were the real deal. Every single one of them had grown up working the family's ranch, and even though they'd gone on to other jobs, professions that took them away from the ranching life, but never too far they couldn't be counted on to lend a hand when needed.

But Dane, he was the real thing. An honest-to-goodness cowboy from the top of his Stetson to the tips of his boots. He worked the ranch, dealt with the day-to-day minutia. Everything from feeding the herd to branding and vaccines, he could and did do it all.

"I kind of inserted myself into said mess, since I'm the one who found the death threat. After that, it was my choice to keep snooping. I just didn't anticipate falling nose deep into a decades' old, real-life murder mystery. Kind of makes me feel like I'm part of the Scooby gang."

Dane chuckled. "Which one are you, Danger-prone Daphne or Velma the Brain?"

"Definitely Velma. She was a total geek girl, so I feel a kinship. After all, geeks shall inherit the earth."

"I always liked Velma. The girl had her own unique style and definitely was the brains of the outfit."

Destiny nodded her agreement. "She definitely knew her way around the facts. So, if I'm Velma, who are you?"

Dane barked a laugh, before answering. "I'm probably

the dog. I feel like I'm bumbling and stumbling my way through things, and every clue I uncover digs me deeper and deeper into a scandal I can't seem to figure out."

"Hey, don't rag on the Scoobster. He was totally underestimated, and always figured the mystery out in the end."

"Somehow I don't think in my case it's going to be the old real estate mogul in a monster mask who ends up the villain in our escapade."

Destiny's heartbeat fluttered in her chest at his use of *our*. Guess he really did intend to let her participate in his private investigation. Not that he could have stopped her, even if he refused to work side-by-side. Her curiosity was piqued. Without a doubt, she had to know the answers, because she couldn't walk away from a puzzle. Especially one involving the hottie in the passenger seat.

"Are you planning on telling Douglas and Ms. Patti?"

Dane scrubbed a hand across his face and gave a weary-sounding sigh. She'd bet he hadn't gotten much sleep the night before either. Then again, after what he'd disclosed to her, that wasn't surprising. Simply thinking about it made her want to turn tail and run because once they started digging deeper, uncovering long-buried secrets, secrets somebody was willing to kill for, it wasn't just Dane's life that would irrevocably change.

"I know I'll have to tell them. Hiding the information from them much longer won't be feasible. I love them you know. I was only six years old when I came to live with them and became part of this amazing family. It was rough, I'm not gonna lie. I was a traumatized kid, ripped away from the only home I'd ever known. I'm quite sure the state labeled me a problem child because I wouldn't talk. Not a word. I'd lived here for six months before I finally spoke."

"I didn't know that. I can't imagine how hard that must have been on you and Douglas and Ms. Patti."

"They both have a well of patience and love that's unending. Douglas never treated me any differently than the others. He simply gave me a safe place to land when I was desperately afraid I'd be cast aside again." A soft smile curved his lips. "Now Momma, on the other hand, she's a nurturer, a born mother. She knew a traumatized, scared child when she saw one. In the beginning, she handled me with kid gloves, doing her best to make me feel safe and secure. She inherently understood my fear of losing my place. Even at six, I knew enough to not get comfortable with the things and places around me, because I'd inevitably be yanked from that reality and into another. But, Momma, she never wavered in her devotion to me. Her determination to make me understand that nothing and nobody would ever take me away. I had my place with the Boudreaus, and she promised me it was okay to settle down. To put down roots, and let them anchor me, not only to the land but to the family."

Destiny blinked back the tears threatening to spill. Dane didn't need to see her cry, especially since he'd opened up and revealed a bit of his childhood. It was not only refreshingly honest, but it made her like him more because of the devotion and love he showed for his parents.

"They adopted you?"

He chuckled, and the sound chased a shiver across her skin. "As fast as was legally possible. Which, as Momma tells it, wasn't nearly quick enough. Of course, there were lots of legal maneuverings that had to be done by the state of Texas, since they had no records or knowledge of who I was or where I came from. I was a ward of the court because there was no record of my parents or any next of kin. Ginger, the woman who'd been taking care of me…well, she wasn't able to give them any information."

Destiny was smart enough to read between the lines. Besides, after her talk with Dane the night before, she'd looked up Ginger Benson when she'd gotten home. The more she'd read about the young woman, the more she'd liked her. She'd also read that Ginger had been killed by an alleged drug dealer during a score that went wrong. Cops had found her body beside a dumpster in a seedy part of Amarillo and closed the case. The police file she'd borrowed—she refused to call it hacking—made no mention of a child. Meaning they had no idea Ginger was taking care of Dane. Her heart ached for the little boy he'd been, alone and scared, with nobody to turn to.

"Anyway, I think we're going to have to come up with a reason to give my parents about why you'll be hanging around my place so much. While we're working on the case.

Otherwise, they are going to get suspicious. And if Nica's home? My sister is nosy as all get out. If she even suspects something's going on, she won't let up until she's got every juicy detail, no matter what it takes."

"I hadn't thought about that. Any suggestions?"

He chuckled and Destiny's heart skipped a beat. *Oh, man, whatever he's about to suggest—it's gonna be a doozy.*

He gave her a beautiful smile. "Just one. Marry me."

CHAPTER FOUR

DANE BARELY BIT back a chuckle as Destiny was swarmed by the women almost as soon as they walked through the front door at the Big House. Everybody seemed to be talking at once, and she shot him a *help me* glare. He simply shrugged and went in search of his dad, who was exactly where he expected him to be. After dropping his bombshell on Destiny as they'd pulled up in front of the Big House, he could guarantee she'd be hunting him down soon enough. He grinned, remembering the look on her face when he'd said those two little words.

Marry me.

Glancing across the backyard patio, he spotted his dad manning the massive outdoor grill. Nobody touched Douglas Boudreau's baby without permission, not even his sons. He'd honed his skills over the years, and everybody in the county wished they were half as good with a side of beef as his dad. There wasn't a doubt in his mind, if he'd gone on the barbecue circuit and entered the competitions, he'd have won.

"Heard you caught a ride back with Destiny."

Ah, that was his father, a man of few words. Yet his point was crystal clear. He wanted to know about Dane's sudden interest in a woman he barely knew, and if there was more to the situation than met the eye. He trusted his father, he truly did, but today wasn't the time or the place to tell him about the secret he'd been keeping his whole life. Something this big needed to be talked about with the whole family in attendance. He also knew when he finally told Momma and Dad, they'd be hurt. Sure, they'd eventually understand and they'd support him one hundred percent in trying to reveal the truth, but it wouldn't stop them from feeling betrayed. Wait, betrayed was too strong a word. But they'd be hurt by his lack of trust. His willful keeping of the story of his life before becoming a Boudreau would shake their bedrock foundation.

Okay, maybe betrayed was the right word after all.

"I like her. She's interesting. Funny. I find her—unique."

"Uh-huh. And you've talked with her how many times?" His dad expertly turned over a couple of steaks, though Dane knew his attention was focused more on the answers he wanted than on the sizzling meat.

"We've chattered several times. As a matter of fact, we went to Juanita's last night."

Douglas' eyes narrowed. "You were at the party with the family last night."

"After I left the party, I met Destiny at Juanita's. Look, Dad, I like her. She's the first woman in a long time who's caught my attention and held it longer than a minute. I want to see where things might go. The only roadblock I'm seeing is her working for Shiloh. The last thing she needs is to worry about her boss haranguing her because she's dating his brother."

"Your brother's probably going to have the same questions I have, because we didn't know you and Destiny were seeing each other, much less wanting to take things seriously. He'll probably have questions because Shiloh tends to be protective about those he considers his. Destiny falls under that shield since she works for him. He considers her a friend."

"As long as he doesn't give her a hard time, I'm cool with it."

He glanced toward the kitchen doorway at the sound of women's voices and spotted Destiny coming out with Tessa and Jill, a large blue bowl in her hands. Meeting her gaze, he saw her helpless shrug as Maggie nudged her with her shoulder and got her moving toward the table already bowing under the weight of all the food.

Gotta love my parents, they know how to feed a crowd.

"Tell your momma what you two are up to, or Destiny's gonna find herself getting the third degree. In the nicest possible way, of course." His dad laughed, his expression filled with love. "Your momma has her own unique way of finding out what she needs to."

"Guess I'd better go rescue her."

"Son." Dane waited for his father to continue. His dad's steadfast gaze held his for several long seconds, and he finally gave a single nod. "Lemme know if there's anything I can do to help."

Trust his dad to cut right straight to the point. He also heard his father's unspoken support, which made him feel warm inside, albeit tinged with guilt. Because he kept secrets. He didn't have a choice—if the truth came out too soon, he wasn't the only person who'd be in danger. No, he'd handle things on his own. Once the threat was contained, and the person responsible for his biological parents' murder behind bars, everything could go back to normal.

"Thanks, Dad."

Walking past the tables practically collapsing under the weight of all the food, he snagged a chocolate chip cookie and took a bite, the taste of brown sugar and chocolate bursting on his tongue. Jill must have made them. Darn, but the woman knew her way around sweets. *How Sweet It Is*, the bakery she'd opened on Main Street, was a huge hit with Shiloh Springs' residents, and she had enough special orders to bring on an additional part-time assistant. Didn't surprise him, not after having eaten her baked goods over the past years. Lucas was a lucky man, having finally pulled his head out of his backside, and proposing to Jill.

"Bro." Shiloh stepped in front of Dane, flanked by Liam and Rafe. Great. Looked like he wasn't going to get a chance to talk to Destiny after all. He only hoped she was able to ward off the onslaught of questions the women would pepper her with, if they hadn't already. He wasn't too worried. Destiny was smart and able to think on her feet. With luck, she'd be able to come up with a plausible story, one he could go along with, embellished with his own twists if need be.

"Gimme a break, guys. We just got here."

"Ah, so you admit it. You brought Destiny with you." Shiloh's tone was more curious than accusatory. He genuinely cared about Destiny. A weird kind of friendship had developed between them when he'd contracted her to work on some side projects. The pretty computer expert originally came to Texas to work for Sentinel Guardians, his brother Ridge's company. She still did contract work for Ridge whenever he needed it, but Destiny and Shiloh seemed to have forged a copacetic working relationship, and she'd gone to work for Shiloh. Guess Shiloh's big brother attitude extended to more than just Nica.

"Why not? She was at church this morning, so I invited her to come and have lunch. It's not a big deal."

"Yeah, I noticed her there, too." Rafe looked across the patio and he smiled. Dane's gaze followed his, noting the women were seated in the area where the loveseat and chairs formed a conversational area, with his mother reigning like the queen she was. Destiny sat on the loveseat between Camilla and Beth, looking like a deer caught in headlights, and he grinned. He'd have to rescue her soon before she bolted.

"Momma said you rode home with her. What's up with that? You barely know her."

Dane shot Shiloh a glare. "What's the big deal, bro? She's a beautiful, single woman. I'm available. Maybe I want to get to know her better."

Shiloh put a hand on his shoulder, squeezing not too gently. "Just take it slow with her. She's been through a lot, and I would hate to see her get hurt."

"I have no intention of hurting Destiny. I like her, at least what I've seen of her." His thoughts went immediately to the day in the Big House's kitchen, when he'd walked in on her showing her tattoo to Tina, swallowing past the sudden lump in his throat.

"Boys, stop giving your brother the third degree." Douglas expertly flipped several burgers on the grill. "He's gonna get enough of that from your momma."

"Great. Think I'll go rescue Destiny."

He walked away before he got roped into another round of the Great Inquisition. Guess he was lucky more of his brothers hadn't gathered around the grill, or he'd have been trapped.

Destiny shot him a *help-me* pleading look. He'd barely made it a few steps forward when an arm ringed around his shoulders, steering him in the opposite direction. An enormous forearm rested against his throat, and he groaned when he spotted Lucas a few feet away. His luck had run out, and he braced himself for another round of questions about him and Destiny. Why, oh why, wasn't he an only child?

SHE'D BEEN SURROUNDED from the moment she stepped through the front door. The hoard had swarmed en masse, descending on her like she was the downed gazelle, and they were the starving lions. Dane was a step behind, but not quick enough to rescue her.

Dragged into the kitchen by Camilla, her hands were filled with a large blue bowl, and she was told to carry it outside. Tessa and Jill flanked her on either side and Destiny smiled at the thought they were her guard dogs, tasked with making sure she didn't make a run for it.

Which sounded like a promising idea at the moment. She already regretted accepting the invitation for lunch at the big house. Though it hadn't been an invitation so much as a demand. When Dane slid onto the passenger seat of her car, she had no choice.

"Come on, slowpoke." Tessa hip-checked Destiny and got her moving through the open doorway. The smell of grilling meat reached her, and her stomach growled. Rumor had it Douglas Boudreau knew his way around a barbecue grill, and if the scents were anything to go by, she was about to have some authentic Texas barbecue. Not the stuff she usually picked up at the chain place, but honest-to-goodness, lick-your-fingers 'cue.

"Put the bowl on the table, and let's sit over there." Jill pointed toward an area across the backyard patio. Upholstered chairs and a loveseat filled the space, giving it a homey, comfortable feel. The arrangement was situated into a conversational area, and she swallowed. Looked like the beef wasn't the only thing being grilled this afternoon.

Sitting on the loveseat, she was immediately flanked by Camilla and Jill, with the other women filling up the adjacent chairs. She tried to brace herself, expecting to be bombarded by questions. Instead, the women talked about Jill's bakery, Camilla's latest book, while Beth patted her obviously pregnant belly. It was all so…normal.

After a few minutes, Ms. Patti joined them, giving Destiny a welcoming smile. Dropping onto the seat directly across from her, Destiny noted the other woman had changed from her church clothes into a soft pink top and white capri pants. Her feet were shod in tennis shoes, and she looked more casual than she'd ever seen the Boudreau matriarch. Relaxed and happy, surrounded by her family, Ms. Patti seemed content with her world, surrounded by those she loved.

"Destiny, I'm so happy you joined us. I've been wanting to get to know you better."

Why does that make me think I better divulge my life history and do it with a smile on my face?

"I'm glad to be here. Ridge and Shiloh both talk about Douglas' skill with a grill. I can't wait to try some."

"Never mind that." Camilla leaned in closer. "You're among friends. Tell us about yourself. Give us all the deets."

Yep, she'd been right. She was about to be subjected to the third degree—by experts.

"Er, not really much to tell. We've talked a couple of times. Nothing serious. Getting to know you stuff."

She looked around, starting to panic a little when she didn't see Dane. Where was he? He really wouldn't abandon her here, alone with—his mother—would he?

Ms. Patti chuckled, reached over and patted Destiny's knee.

"The look of panic on your face. Hon, don't worry, I promise your interrogation will be mostly painless."

Destiny blew out the breath she'd been holding. What was she worried about? There's no way Ms. Patti or anybody else knew about her. Her past was a closed book, a chapter she never looked at or thought about. Let Ms. Patti and the crew do their worst; they wouldn't break her.

"We've all been through this." Camilla leaned in and whispered. "Trust me, if you like Dane, it'll be worth it."

"True." This from Jill.

"You're originally from California?"

"Yes, ma'am. Lived there most of my life. I moved here last year when I took the job working for Ridge."

Ms. Patti nodded. "I know he was sorry to lose you.

How's it been, working with my other son?"

"Shiloh's been amazing to work with. He allows me to do my own thing, at my pace, as long as I produce results. And I always get the information he needs. I'm good at what I do. Plus, he doesn't care when I take on contract work for Ridge from time to time. As long as it doesn't interfere with any open cases I'm working on, he's cool with it."

"How is it we're just getting to know you better, hmm? You've been here a year, work for two of my sons, and yet I feel like I barely know you. We definitely have to change that."

Beth raised her hand and waved, getting Destiny's attention. "I second that. I'd really like to get to know you. I've got tons of questions. Nosy, prying questions." She grinned and patted her belly again. "Kiddo's kicking up a storm today. I think he or she agrees about wanting to get to know you." She looked down at her stomach. "Just not too soon. You stay put."

"There is a plus side to sharing information, you know." Jill popped a piece of cookie into her mouth and chewed. "It works both ways. We get to ask you all sorts of prying questions, but you're allowed to do the same. Kind of a tit-for-tat. You want to know something, ask."

"Really?"

All the women nodded, even Ms. Patti. This might be interesting after all. There was a ton of information she could glean from digging online but getting it straight from the horse's mouth. That was pure gold.

Leaning back against the cushions of the loveseat, she relaxed.

"Ladies, I'm an open book. Ask away."

CHAPTER FIVE

"YOU ABANDONED ME."

Dane raised his hands at her accusation, as if warding off her verbal blow. "Wasn't my fault, I swear. I went to talk to my dad for a second, and then got ambushed by my brothers."

"Well, let me tell you, cowboy, your future sisters-in-law make the Spanish Inquisition look like a tea party. I'd barely answered one question before another one was lobbed at me like a hand grenade. It was like a tag-team event. When one finished, the next one grilled me."

Destiny flung herself onto the sofa in Dane's living room. They'd left the family lunch a few minutes earlier, and she'd driven them to the foreman's house, knowing Dane was right: they needed to get their stories straight. She was still reeling from his marriage proposal earlier. If that could be called a proposal. Did he seriously think his family and friends would back off if they got hitched? And why? Why couldn't she simply move in with him for a few weeks, until they figured out Dane's dilemma, and then go back to her regular life?

"I've got a couple of reasons for suggesting we get married."

Oops, she hadn't realized she'd spoken out loud until he answered. She'd have to watch that, because it was a bad habit, and had gotten her in trouble more than once in the past.

"I can't think of a single good explanation, but I'm all ears, cowboy."

"First, this is small-town Texas. Conservative, family-oriented. People don't simply move in together when they barely know each other."

She quirked her brow. "So they get married instead?"

"In my family they do. Not that I wouldn't live with somebody if I cared about them. There are also my parents to consider."

"Which ones?" She regretted the question the moment it left her mouth.

Dang it, I did it again. Open mouth, insert foot.

Dane handed her the mug of coffee, and then dropped onto the other end of the couch, his own mug in hand. She wrapped her hands around it, letting the warmth settle her like a gentle hug. While she'd never admit it out loud, she was nervous. And she never got nervous around guys. They were friends. Buddies. Co-workers. But with Dane, it felt—different.

"There are a couple of reasons why marriage is the best option. First, it'll stop any wagging tongues from spreading gossip. If you moved in with me, the news would spread like a prairie fire and only grow in intensity. There would be whispers and innuendos that wouldn't die away easily."

"I don't care what others think about me."

"And if all I had to consider was me, I'd curse them all to hades and be done with it. My family, on the other hand, they'll get caught in the crosshairs of the rumor mill. Since this is my problem, they shouldn't have to face the blowback of my actions. Especially because the people I'm going against are rich and powerful, and if they had my parents killed, they won't stop at going after my adoptive family."

She nodded, taking a sip of coffee. The slightly bitter brew slid down like an old friend. It was her vice, her addiction of choice. She downed gallons of the stuff when she was working. At times she had a perpetual buzz from all the caffeine she wallowed in.

"I understand. It'll make things harder, but I don't have to move in. We could manage to work this investigation remotely."

"We could. It might work, but with the threat hanging over my head, time is of the essence. Working separately will slow things down. Besides, if anybody finds out you're collaborating with me on bringing down my parents' killer, they could target you, too."

"I know. It's a risk I'm willing to take."

"I'm not." Dane's voice gritted like rocks grinding together, each word rough and jagged. "It's an all-in or nothing proposition. If you're going to work with me, we're together. Living under the same roof where I can watch your back."

Destiny sat up straight and gently placed the coffee mug on the side table. "Only if it works both ways, cowboy. You watch my back. I'll watch yours." When he started to interrupt, she pointed a finger at him. "I'm trained. Probably better than you are. I have a black belt in Brazilian Jiu-Jitsu. I've studied Krav Maga. I'm a proficient shot, and I have a concealed carry permit for the state of Texas. Maybe you should just hire me to be your bodyguard."

Dane grinned, the tiny lines at the corners of his eyes crinkling with mirth. "I'm impressed, princess. Guess you're not just a pretty face."

Destiny felt heat rise in her cheeks at his compliment. Being around Dane Boudreau seemed to keep her off balance. She wasn't the blushing type, far from it. She'd learned long ago not to be ruled by her emotions, and not to care what others thought about her. Yet Dane's approval gave her all kinds of warm and fuzzy feelings. She shook her head, banishing the wayward thought.

"You said there was another reason for getting married."

"Yes." He scooted forward to the edge of the sofa, and reached for her hand, wrapping his warm fingers around hers. "You know who I'm going after. Why it has to be done. If I'm right—"

"You are," she interrupted. "All the evidence points to you being right."

"If I'm right, we are talking about a lot of money being at stake. People with money will sometimes do anything to keep it. I want to make certain my parents' inheritance goes where it was intended. If anything happens to me, as my wife you'd inherit."

"But—"

Dane continued as if she hadn't said a word. "I'll make sure my will is updated, so you'd inherit everything except this house. It has to stay part of the Boudreau property. You understand that, right?"

"Of course." She drew in a ragged breath. His bold statement hit her like a punch to the chest, right over her heart. Such an honorable man, she knew he'd do what was right, no matter what. Once again, she was seeing the cumulative effect of being raised by Douglas and Patti Boudreau. Their influence and guidance had honed and shaped Dane into an upstanding man, determined to make things right for his biological family, no matter what the cost.

Even if that cost was his life.

"Matthew MacKenna runs MacKenna-Duncan International. He'll have a coterie of the highest-paid lawyers in the country at his beck and call. Probably enough to find a loophole to prevent my adoptive family from inheriting. You're a lady, so I won't use the words I'd like to describe the piece of garbage. But all the research shows he's ruthless when it comes to MacKenna-Duncan International, and he'll stop at nothing to keep it."

"Dane, maybe we need to think this through. Matthew MacKenna was your father's best friend. His business partner. From what I read, he is your godfather."

"And he's likely the person responsible for murdering my parents." Dane released her hand and stood, pacing to stand in front of the huge limestone fireplace. The enormous pieces of Texas limestone made a splendid backdrop for Dane's rugged good looks, emphasizing his muscled body, which years of ranching had honed to perfection.

"Douglas and Ms. Patti will stand beside you, fight for your rights to finding the truth. I think you should tell them."

"Tell them what? That I've always known who I was? Tell them I was there when my parents were killed when I was six years old? The truth is going to hurt because they'll think I didn't trust them enough, or I didn't love them enough to tell them. They won't understand that I didn't tell them because I was protecting them."

Standing, she walked over and without thinking about it, wrapped her arms around him, pulling him against her. She'd never seen anybody who needed a hug more. The warmth of human contact. The feeling of being connected. Because she understood where he was at—in his head and his heart—and while she didn't necessarily agree, she'd give him what comfort she could.

She felt him take a deep breath, and after what seemed

eons, his arms wrapped around her, squeezing her tight. Simply being in his arms, resting her head against his shoulder, sent a wave of peace through her, and she prayed she gave him the same sense of comfort. It hurt her heart to know he agonized over how his parents would feel when they found out the truth he'd hidden most of his life. Personally, though she didn't know them well, she believed they'd forgive him and do everything in their power to make sure justice prevailed for his slain biological parents.

Add in the fact that his brothers could help—well, that only muddied the waters. A sheriff, an FBI agent, a DEA agent, another who owned a security company (and who was also her boss), along with an investigative reporter who was known for exposing corruption? It all added up to all the help he'd ever need—and they were going to be royally perturbed he hadn't asked them for help a long time ago.

Reluctantly, she lowered her arms and stepped back, immediately feeling the loss of warmth and connection. She didn't understand this primal urge to be near Dane. The overwhelming instinct to touch him. Comfort him. Heal him. It had never happened before with anybody, and it scared her. Because she knew, if she let herself, she'd fall for the handsome rancher.

"Do you honestly think marrying me will help?" Her words were soft, almost a whisper, and she was afraid he didn't hear them.

"I do."

Smirking, she shot back. "Save those words for the ceremony, cowboy."

She watched as his expression cleared, and a huge grin curved his sexy mouth. "Does that mean you're saying yes?"

"Heaven help me, I'm saying yes. I think we're both insane and this is going to backfire spectacularly, but I'm all in. Let's get married."

DANE WATCHED THE taillights of Destiny's car as it pulled away, standing in solitude on the front porch. An inexplicable feeling of contentment filled him, and he leaned against the doorjamb, going over the plans they'd made in the last hour.

I can't believe she said yes.

Stepping back inside, he pulled his cellphone from his pocket and dialed his number one ranch hand. Domenico Juarez had worked on the Boudreau spread for the past five years and had proven his dependability and loyalty, quickly moving up through the hierarchy to be his go-to man for getting things done. All the hands knew they could go to Dom with any problems, and he'd get things handled. Now, Dane was going to need him more than ever, since he'd have to turn the day-to-day running of the ranch over to him for the next few weeks.

"Hey, Dane. What's up?"

"Dom, I'm going to need a rather huge favor. One that entails you taking on some added responsibilities. You game?"

"Of course. Whatever you need."

Dane chuckled at the eagerness in the other man's voice. Only a couple of years younger than him, Dom soaked up information like a sponge, ready and willing to take on any task, to master any skill, because he had aspirations and dreams of owning his own spread by the time he was forty. Dane didn't doubt Dom could and would make it happen.

"Listen, I'm going to need you to run the place for a few weeks. Deal with any issues that arise. I won't be available unless it's an emergency. By that, I mean a crisis. Like biblical flood-type destruction. Think you can oversee things?"

"Are you kidding?" The incredulous shock gave way to excitement, as what Dane was asking sank in. "I'm your guy. The crew knows their job. The vet's not scheduled for a couple weeks, so we're okay there. Branding shouldn't be a problem, since we picked up a couple new hands last week."

"That's what I was hoping you'd say. There's one other thing though, Dom. You cannot tell anybody I'm not around. As far as everybody's concerned, if they come looking for me, I'm somewhere on the ranch. Make up a story if you have to about where I'm at. Just as long as they don't know I've taken off for a few days, everything should be fine."

There was a long moment of silence on the other end, and for a second Dane wondered if Dom changed his mind. While officially he worked for the Boudreau Ranch, technically the corporation was owned by his parents. Maybe Dom would have a problem lying to them, afraid he'd lose his position.

"What about your folks? They ask where you're at, what am I supposed to tell 'em?"

"Dom, I'm going to tell you something, and you cannot repeat it. Not to anybody, but especially not to my family. Got it?"

"Um—sure."

Dane flung himself onto the sofa and placed his feet on the coffee table. "I'm getting married."

"Married? Dude, I didn't even know you were dating." Shock colored Dom's voice.

"We've kept it a secret. Didn't want to say anything until we were sure it was meant to be."

It's meant to be alright. Meant to help me uncover a killer.
"Who is she?"

"Nobody you know. Here's the thing, the reason I need you to cover for me. We're eloping. Before you say anything, we talked about it and decided we don't want all the frou-frou stuff. Momma and the family would insist on a big church wedding and reception, and that's not what we want. So, we're going to find a quiet place to say our vows, and when we come home, it will be a done deal."

Dom let out a low whistle. "Your mother is not going to be happy, my man. With all your brothers getting engaged, and all these weddings in the works, she's got wedding fever."

"Exactly. She thinks all her sons should have these extravagant shindigs and all I want is just us. Later, after the shock wears off, we'll have a nice family party with our friends. Of course, you'll be invited."

Dane pinched the bridge of his nose, feeling the beginning of a headache behind his eyes. The lack of sleep the past few nights had him cranky and ill-tempered, and he wanted to grab a few hours of shuteye before heading to the airport with Destiny. But there were plans to make, things that needed handling personally before he allowed himself to be whisked away to his whirlwind wedding.

"Dane Boudreau married. Never thought I'd see the day. You haven't mentioned anybody special, so you've blindsided me with this news. Of course I'll cover for you. Let's just hope your folks don't come round asking questions, because it won't sit right with me, lying to 'em."

"I promise I won't let any of my actions blow back onto you. As far as I'm concerned, your job is safe."

"Good to know, dude, but just so you know, I've always got your back. Job or no job, you're my friend, and I've got your back."

"Thanks, Dom. You ever need me, I'm here for you, too."

There was a short pause on the line, then Dom's voice came back. "I've gotta ask, man. Is she hot?"

Dane smiled, picturing Destiny in his head, her short dark hair surrounding her face. Big blue eyes filled with mischief and a genuine sense of joy. The brilliantly colored tattoo just above her left breast. Was she hot?

"You have no idea."

CHAPTER SIX

DESTINY COULDN'T STOP fiddling with the zipper on her backpack. Sliding it open, she checked for the hundredth time to make sure her computer, power cord, and the handwritten files were inside. She glanced at the other bag sitting by the front door, the one containing her clothing and other stuff.

For my wedding day.

"I've lost my ever-loving mind. How did I let Dane talk me into this insanity?"

She knew why. Because it was nearly impossible to say no to the man. Helping him dig up information on his family? No problem. Working with him to take down a multibillion-dollar corporation? Piece of cake. Saying no to his marriage proposal?

Impossible.

She jumped at the brief rap on her front door, and her heartbeat revved like the motor on an Indy car. On the other side of that door stood her future husband. The man who in a few short hours would be hers—for better or worse.

Looping the backpack's strap over her shoulder, she

reached for the doorknob and twisted it, pulling the door inward. Dane stood in the apartment building's hall, dressed in dark wash jeans and a black T-shirt, holding a dark-colored Stetson in his right hand. His hair was disheveled, like he'd been running his fingers through it, and she barely resisted the urge to reach up and brush the strands off his forehead.

"Good morning." It felt like her tongue was glued to the roof of her mouth, and the words came out muffled, and she wanted to slink through the floorboards. Perfect way to start her wedding day.

Ugh, I've got to stop thinking about today as my wedding day. It's a business transaction, plain and simple. It doesn't mean anything. A means to an end, to keep bad people from hurting the Boudreaus.

"Hi. You ready? We've got a long drive to the airport."

Dane spotted her bag sitting just inside the doorway, and leaned forward and grabbed it, lifting it like it weighed nothing.

"Airport? I thought we'd just drive over into Louisiana or Oklahoma and do the deed."

Smooth, Destiny. Do the deed? Can I sound any more pathetic?

"I've booked us on a flight to Las Vegas."

"Vegas? Seriously? Is Elvis performing our ceremony?" She couldn't help smiling when she spotted his grin.

"I can make that happen if you want."

"Nope. I think a simple justice of the peace will do." Sliding past Dane into the hall, she pulled the door closed and locked it, shoving the keys into her pocket before turning to face him. "Can I ask, why Vegas?"

Dane started toward the stairs and Destiny sped up, trying to keep up with his long-legged gait. It didn't help that the view of him walking in front of her was so tantalizing. Firm muscles in his shoulders moved with a sinewy grace, leading to a narrow waist and slim hips. Altogether, it was a delicious package, one she wanted to indulge in.

She gave herself a mental slap upside the head. *Bad Destiny. Stop staring at the hot cowboy. This is business. All business. No pleasure. Keep your mind out of the gutter and—*

"Oomph." Destiny rocked back on her heels after slamming into Dane's back. She hadn't been paying attention, too busy watching her fantasy hunk of beefcake, and now paid the price. "Sorry."

"No problem, princess. In answer to your question, we're going to Vegas because that's where Matthew MacKenna is going to be."

Ah-ha, now she understood Dane's rush to head west. "What's he doing in Vegas? Last I checked, he was tied up with the takeover of Rice Industries. A not-so-happy acquisition from what I gleaned. Shouldn't he be handholding the stockholders, spouting the *everything's going to stay the same* spiel?"

"One of my informants told me MacKenna is meeting

with Malcolm Winters. Closed-door, confidential meeting. I know where they are staying and thought we might be able to do some undercover work, fill in a few blanks while we're there."

She ran the name around in her head, knowing Malcolm Winters factored into the research she'd done after discovering the contract on Dane's life. Winters might be well-respected in the business community, but his reputation beneath the surface wasn't so squeaky clean. He'd been known to cut more than a few corners in building his construction empire. Shoddy workmanship, low-quality materials in place of high-end finishes, and failure to enforce contractual obligations were just a few of the accusations leveled at the man. There'd also been unsubstantiated whispers of mob connections. After looking at his pictures online, seeing the hardness in his eyes the camera didn't disguise, that allegation seemed more fact than fiction.

The elevator doors opened to the lobby, and they stepped out. Destiny loved her complex's front common area. Spacious and larger than you'd expect when viewing it from the outside, there was a bank of windows on either side of the entrance. Natural light spilled onto the patterned floor. When coming in, the elevator was across from the big double doors. To the right was a gym and weight room, one of the perks included in her rent. To the left was a long corridor with rentable office spaces and at the end of the hall was one of the best perks. A large outdoor pool had been added when the owner purchased a parcel of land that sat adjacent to the building.

Her apartment building was an old office space, three floors that had been converted into apartments, each one either two or three bedrooms. She'd lucked into one of the two-bedroom units, setting one up as her home office. She didn't need to have a guest room. There wasn't anybody coming to visit, and an office made more sense, given the odd hours she often worked for Shiloh.

"I remember my dad's company working on this place. Turned out pretty good."

"Your father did the construction work?"

Dane smiled. "You might say that. Did it as a favor to Momma. She owns the building."

"What? Your mother is my landlord?" How had she not realized that when she moved in?

"In a roundabout way, I guess she is. Buying and selling real estate is her main focus, but she's got a couple of income-producing properties she invested in. There's a holding company that oversees and manages them. She's not involved in the day-to-day running, if that's what's bothering you. Chances are she doesn't even know you're living in one of her buildings."

Destiny shot him a side-eye glance. "We're talking about Patti Boudreau, right? That woman knows everything that's going on in Shiloh Springs and I wouldn't be surprised if she doesn't have her finger on the pulse of every town surrounding it. Nothing escapes her eagle eye."

He shrugged and held open the front door. Destiny spotted his pickup truck parked at the curb, instead of in guest parking. Shaking her head, she reached for the door handle, but Dane's reached it before she'd even touched the metal. Cowboy had good manners; she'd hand him that. Sliding onto the seat, she buckled in, stowing her backpack on the floor between her feet.

Dane walked around to the other side, after stowing her other bag in the truck bed. Within a minute they were off, effortlessly merging onto the highway not far from her place. They rode in companionable silence, and she watched the long stretches of land dotted with billboards advertising everything from restaurants and gas stations to small-town tourist activities. The soft hum of country music played in the truck's cab, a soothing white noise in the background. She felt her eyelids start drifting closed.

The ringing of her phone startled her, and she winced when she saw her boss' name on the screen.

"Hey, Shiloh."

"What's this about you taking time off? Is everything okay?" Concern laced his words, and guilt tightened her core. She hated lying to him. Shiloh's twin brother, Ridge, took a chance on her when she'd been in a tight spot back in California, giving her not only a new job, but a chance at starting her life over. He hadn't protested overly much when she'd decided to switch jobs and work for Shiloh after a few months, as long as she did the occasional contract job for him. Now, because of her helping Dane, she had to keep a secret from her friend.

"I'm good. Just had some unexpected personal stuff come up, something I have to handle in person. I'll be gone for a few days. I gave all my info on the Stevens case to Jim. Shouldn't take him any time to get up to speed."

"You know if you need anything, all you've got to do is ask, right?"

She smiled. "I know. Have I mentioned what a great boss you are?"

"Not nearly often enough. Call me if I can help in any way."

"I will. Thanks, Shiloh."

Disconnecting the call, she shoved the phone in her pocket. "I hate lying to your brother."

"You can always back out. As long as you don't tell anybody what I'm up to, I'll turn around and take you back home." Dane glanced over at her, before turning his attention back to the road. He drove with a confidence Destiny envied. She disliked being stuck inside a car and took her motorcycle everywhere she could. If she had her way, she'd never drive a car again. It wasn't that she was a bad driver; she wasn't. She hated being confined inside the cramped space. Given her druthers, she'd much rather feel the wind in her face, the freedom of being on two wheels speeding along an open road.

"You're not getting rid of me that easy, buster. We do this together. So get the thought of ditching me out of your head."

Leaning back, she turned to stare out the window. A few minutes passed before Dane slowed, heading for an exit marked rest area. He pulled the pickup into a stop, parking far away from a couple of other cars, and people seated at the picnic tables.

"Before this goes any further, I have to tell you something."

"Okay."

He shifted in his seat until he was facing her. "A couple of weeks ago somebody took a shot at me."

"Dane!"

"I know, I should have said something when you found out about the contract on my life, but…" He trailed off and she wanted to hit him. How could he keep something like that secret, especially with everything she'd shared with him? All the stuff on the internet, especially the fact a mercenary had accepted the contract on his life.

"Tell me everything. When did it happen? How, why?"

"I was out looking for strays. Riding the UTV, in case I needed to carry one back. Occasionally I'll find an injured or abandoned calf and loading it in the back of the UTV is easier than trying to hold it while I'm on the back of a horse."

"Uh-huh. I don't know what a UTV is, but keep going."

"Utility terrain vehicle, good for hauling stuff on a ranch. On that day, I hadn't found any strays but did find a couple of fence posts knocked over. I got out to stand them upright and heard a sound. I've been around guns enough to recognize the sound for what it was, so I ducked down behind the UTV and grabbed the rifle I keep behind the seat. After a couple minutes, I didn't hear anything else. I stood up and looked around. Didn't find anything except a bullet hole."

"And you didn't tell me this when I told you about the hit? Or any time since then? We've only been working to figure out how to stop whoever's trying to kill you and prove who murdered your parents."

She huffed out a breath and crossed her arms over her chest. It felt like a betrayal, him not telling her. Granted, they weren't best buds or anything, but they were working for a common goal—to keep his stupid backside alive and kicking. Right now, she felt more like kicking it herself.

"I'm telling you now. It might have been nothing. In the country, we hear shots all the time. Hunters poaching in places they shouldn't be. Idiots doing target practice in areas they don't belong. It was only one shot; it could mean nothing. But, since we're about to accelerate the fight to get justice for my parents, I thought you should know. Because if it wasn't an accident, a stray bullet, you need to pay attention, be on alert when you're near me."

"Thanks for the warning, but I know what I'm getting

into. I can take care of myself."

"I never doubted that for an instance. I just wanted to give you one last chance to change your mind, because once you get on the plane, there's no turning back."

She looked out the pickup's window, watching the families at the picnic tables laughing and joking, being together. Free from worrying about a hired hitman trying to take them out, because of circumstances outside their control. Let Dane think she was considering backing out, but her mind had been made up the minute she'd clicked on the mercenary website listing Dane's name. There was no changing her mind.

"You'd better get this truck back on the highway or we're going to miss our flight."

Without a word, Dane started the engine and pulled back onto the roadway. Looked like she was headed to Las Vegas—and marriage to Dane Boudreau.

CHAPTER SEVEN

D ESTINY SMOOTHED HER hands along the skirt of the dress she'd found waiting for her when she'd checked into her room. They'd come straight from the airport, checking into the Bellagio, right on the Vegas strip. The view from her window gave her a perfect view of the dancing fountains, a spectacle she'd never expected to see in person. The sparkling lights reflecting on the water, the movements a sinuous delight, matched the fluttering in her stomach. A kaleidoscope of colors, fascinating the senses, she found herself wondering why Dane picked this place for their stay. While she appreciated the luxuries in life, same as anybody, they weren't a necessity. She got by quite well with four walls and a roof, as long as she had her computer and good Wi-Fi.

She'd found the elegantly wrapped package sitting on the foot of the bed, the white and silver ribbons and paper beckoning to her, and she couldn't resist it. The box called to her like a siren's song, luring her, its tantalizing allure capturing her in its web. Quickly pulling the ribbons free, she folded back the tissue paper, uncovering the beautiful off-white dress, a sheath dress underneath with an overlay of lace. Holding it up in front of her, she twirled in front of the mirror, and for a moment, she'd allowed herself to believe this wedding was the real thing.

The dress fit like it was made for her, hugging each curve. The exquisite lace was soft, the color perfectly suiting her skin tone. She'd almost missed the envelope tucked into the neckline of the garment, the color nearly identical to the dress. Inside, a brief note stated Dane wanted her to wear the dress to the wedding, which was taking place in a little over an hour. A silver locket slid free from the envelope, a delicate filigree pattern with a stylized capital B entwined into the design.

B for Boudreau.

Good thing she'd brought along a pair of white sandals to wear with the lone dress she'd packed to get married in, otherwise she'd have ended up wearing her black high tops to the ceremony. Definitely would've made the whole ensemble more interesting, she thought. Since she wasn't a girly girl, worrying about her hair and makeup on most days, she simply ran a brush through her short hair, tugging at the chunky pieces to give it a semblance of style. A quick brush of mascara on her lashes and a light pink lip gloss and she was as ready as she was going to be.

A hard knock on the door had her turning from the window. She knew who'd be on the other side. The man soon to be her husband.

I can do this. It's just another job. Nothing personal. Get the job done, let the cops deal with the fallout, then go home and get on with my life.

Opening the door, her breath caught in the back of her throat when she looked at Dane. He'd opted not to go for the whole suit and tie, but his dark-washed jeans looked new and crisp, and the color of his shirt was a close match for her dress. A couple of buttons were open at the neck, exposing just enough of his chest to make her swallow the sudden lump in her throat.

"Hi." Her voice came out in a breathless whisper.

"Hi yourself. You look beautiful." His gaze roamed over her like a physical caress, and she was glad she'd taken a few minutes to fix herself up a little. From his smile, he liked what he saw.

"You clean up pretty well yourself, Mr. Boudreau. Thank you for the dress. It's beautiful." Her fingers fluttered upward to touch the pendant he'd given her.

"We need to head out if we're going to make our appointment time. You ready?"

Without a word she grabbed her wallet and stuffed the room's keycard inside. "Let's go."

Within minutes, they arrived at the chapel where Dane had arranged for their ceremony. It wasn't anything fancy or gaudy. No chance of Elvis performing the ceremony here; it looked more like a little country church than something you'd find in the heart of Las Vegas.

Walking inside, Destiny couldn't help smiling. She'd

been totally wrong. The inside most definitely didn't match the outside. While staid and sedate judging from the exterior, indoors was a game changer. A group of people, obviously guests of the couple waiting for their ceremony to begin, were dressed as characters from The Rocky Horror Picture Show. In full color costumes and makeup, each partygoer played their part to the hilt, with the bride and groom as the strait-laced, stranded motorists, Brad and Janet, in their underwear.

Leaning toward Dane, she whispered, "I think we're overdressed."

"I'm thinking we're in the wrong movie."

An older woman eased past the costumed partiers, to stand in front of them, a notebook in her hands. "Mr. Boudreau and Ms. Smith?"

"Yes."

"If you'll follow me, the reverend is ready for you."

Following the woman, and leaving the boisterous crowd behind, Destiny watched wide-eyed as they walked down a hall, the walls covered with photos of what had to be couples who'd been married here. Each one seemed unique in their own way, varying from simple and sweet to elaborate and over-the-top.

When they reached a cordoned-off area, behind an honest to goodness red velvet rope, they stopped. The woman motioned them over to a small desk and pulled papers out of her notebook.

"I'll need your signatures on these, so we can get you married." Pointing to each, she said, "Sign here, and here, and here."

Destiny twisted her fingers together, over and over, watching Dane sign, his signature bold and strong. Just like him. There was no hesitation, no second-guessing their decision. He handed her the pen, and she took a deep breath, adding her signature on the line beneath his.

No turning back now.

"Don't worry, honey, a bit of nerves is completely normal in a young bride. Before you know it, you'll be the wife of this handsome young man, and be ready to start the rest of your life together."

"Thanks but I'm fine." Her gaze caught Dane's. "Really. Let's get married."

A tall, thin man entered through a side door, and Destiny hoped she didn't gape, but the sight of him was startling. He had to be at least seven feet tall and was skinny as a post. Wearing a black suit and tie, with a white shirt, his balding head shone under the bright lights. He reminded her of a character from one of those sixties monster shows, though she couldn't remember his name.

Can this night get any weirder? First we got Dr. Frank-N-Furter, and now we've got Lurch. That was it, Lurch! Well at least my first wedding is memorable.

Taking their place at the front of the chapel space, beneath the trellis arch festooned with white silk flowers, they spoke their vows. Because she hadn't had time to prepare, they went with the regular vows, and she gave her word to love and honor Dane, forsaking all others. The words rang true as she spoke them, and she felt as if she made a lifelong commitment to the man standing before her. It didn't feel like make-believe. It didn't feel like a job or a means to an end.

It felt like she pledged her life and her love to Dane Boudreau.

When he repeated his vows, Destiny felt them to the depth of her soul, wishing he meant them. It was crazy because she barely knew him, yet she wished with every part of her being that this wedding was real.

"You may now kiss your bride."

Destiny's head jerked up at the reverend's words. Kiss him? That wasn't something she'd considered. When Dane leaned toward her, she closed her eyes, ready to feel his lips brush against hers in a barely-there kiss, enough to satisfy the reverend and their witness.

Only that's not what happened.

Dane's mouth devoured hers. Her gasp of shock was swallowed by his lips, and she melted into his arms when her knees threatened to buckle beneath her. This was more than a simple kiss. It was an assault on her senses, and everything around her disappeared. The only thing real, the only thing she could cling to, was Dane's kiss.

An almost inaudible clicking sound pulled her back, and

she broke free from the hypnotic kiss. Dane looked almost as shocked as she felt, and her fingers brushed against her lips, her gaze locked with his.

"Here you go, Mr. Boudreau. Congratulations." The woman who witnessed their ceremony handed a cell phone to Dane. "I took a couple of pictures during the ceremony and one of the kiss at the end. They look beautiful. If you like, you can e-mail them to yourselves."

"Thank you. I appreciate it. We wanted to have a couple of candid shots of the ceremony, to show our family." Dane took the phone and passed a handful of bills to the woman, quickly downloading the pictures.

"May your marriage be long and happy, Mr. and Mrs. Boudreau."

Mrs. Boudreau. She was really Mrs. Dane Boudreau. The heady reality swirled through her mind.

Dane's hand wrapped around hers, and they walked back to the front, where the group from Rocky Horror still milled around the front entrance. Their bright costumes and happy, carefree attitude were contagious, and Destiny smiled as the group sang one of the songs from the movie.

"Want to see if they'll take a couple of pictures with us before we leave? I'd love to see my brothers' faces when they see those."

Destiny grinned at the thought of Shiloh's face, seeing her and Dane with the cast of Rocky Horror. Plus, it would give her some great memories, for after the marriage was over.

"I'm game if they are."

After a quick discussion, Destiny and Dane were surrounded by the costumed and heavily made-up characters, snapping photos on Dane's phone, and having a blast. Everyone was friendly, outgoing, and the impromptu photo/wedding session ended far too quickly for Destiny.

"You hungry?"

Destiny's stomach took that moment to rumble and she shrugged. "I could eat."

"I know a Japanese Teppanyaki place that has great food. Sound good?"

"I haven't had Japanese in forever. Teppanyaki, that's where they cook at the table, right? I've never done that."

"So, it'll be a new experience for you today."

"Today's been full of new experiences. What's one more?"

Dane laughed and reached over to squeeze her hand. "Yeah, it's been a day of firsts. Tell you what, let's forget about everything for the rest of the night. No business. No Shiloh Springs. Let's just have a good dinner."

Little fluttering motions started low in Destiny's belly at his low-voiced suggestion. She knew he didn't mean anything by it, simply sharing a meal, but she decided to steal this moment, add it to her memory box because it would probably be the only time she'd get with her husband.

Her husband.

Walking into the restaurant, Destiny was doubly glad she wore a higher-end dress because this was no hole-in-the-wall place. Dinner here probably cost more than she made in a month.

"Dane, I don't think—"

"Princess, let me do this. You only have one wedding dinner, so let's make it special."

"We can't make this more than business, Dane. If we allow emotions to cloud things—"

Dane's hands landed gently on her shoulders, and he stared into her eyes. His serious expression told her more than words he understood her meaning all too well.

"I know. We've got a job to do. And we will. I wanted to, I don't know, have a special night, a special memory, before we take the next step that could take us down a path there's no returning from."

Hoping she wasn't making a huge mistake because she was already in danger of losing her heart to her cowboy, she gave him a timid smile.

"I love the idea. Let's make it a night to remember."

THE PHONE RANG and rang, making him antsy. Brian wasn't happy with this job, didn't like the lack of details, or the sketchy background information he'd been provided. He especially didn't like horning in on somebody's wedding night. Following Dane Boudreau to Vegas had been an unexpected move, and he'd been playing catch up for hours. Who knew the man could move so fast, once he decided on a course of action? He'd even flown to Vegas on the same flight, and kept following him from place to place. It was getting tiring.

Who knew the man planned to elope with Destiny Smith? According to his files, he wasn't even seriously dating anyone. The beautiful brunette at his side was an unknown commodity, one he should have known about. Somebody at the FBI had fallen down on the job, and the lack of information galled. He prided himself on being fully informed before taking on a job, but he wasn't turning down anything connected to the Boudreaus. This assignment so far had been nothing but a joke. Nothing was as it seemed, and it was starting to hack him off.

"Hello." The greeting was abrupt, unemotional. Mr. Moneybags might be paying a small fortune for this job, but he wasn't the best conversationalist.

"I'm a very unhappy man. Your report left out more than a few salient details."

"Impossible. My team—"

Brian interrupted. "Your team is obviously comprised of a bunch of incompetent buffoons. Dane Boudreau is in Vegas."

A string of curses filled his ears. Good, maybe his employer now realized the gravity of not providing him with all the pertinent information to complete a successful job. Wouldn't it be interesting if Dane Boudreau managed to run into his current employer, who happened to be in Vegas too? Coincidence?

I don't believe in coincidences.

"What's Boudreau doing in Vegas?"

"Getting married. He's eloping with a pretty brunette named Destiny Smith."

"What!"

That's right, jerk, guess you don't know everything.

"I said he's eloped. I managed to catch up with them after the ceremony, so I can't provide any pictures. I followed them to a local restaurant, where they're currently dining. Guess they weren't in a hurry to get to the wedding night."

"What restaurant?" Looked like his employer was finally taking the information seriously. Brian rattled off the name of the Japanese restaurant where he currently sat, his view unobstructed of Dane Boudreau and his new bride. Watched them smile and whisper, and he had to admit he wished he was close enough to hear. Wondered if Dane Boudreau had any idea he was being stalked, hunted like prey. The bounty on his head would have attracted every two-bit wannabe mercenary with delusions of being the next great assassin in a world of two-bit killers.

"How much does he know?"

Does this guy seriously expect an answer?

"You're the one having his every keystroke monitored. You tell me."

There was a long moment of silence on the other end. Maybe he'd gone too far with his sarcastic comeback, but Brian had grown tired of his current boss' incredible ego and ineptitude. Half the time the information he provided was incomplete or outdated.

"Don't overstep your usefulness. Remember who you're talking to."

Like I'm going to forget. I wish I'd never taken on this job. My real bosses are going to owe me an all-expense paid vacation to a nice sunny beach somewhere once we throw your sorry backside in prison.

"Keep your eyes on them. Find out what he's up to and how much he knows. I'm paying you a lot of money. Don't make me regret hiring you. You won't like the way I terminate our contract."

Without another word, he disconnected the call.

Guess I'm still on the clock. For now.

Popping a shrimp into his mouth, he leaned back and decided to enjoy the show. And he didn't mean the one being given by the chef performing at his table.

No, he was far more interested in the show taking place a few tables away. The one starring Dane Boudreau.

CHAPTER EIGHT

DANE'S ENTIRE BODY went rigid when he spotted the figure walking through the door of the restaurant. Unbelievable. He'd known Matthew MacKenna was in Vegas. It had been the deciding factor for choosing it when making his plans to marry Destiny. He'd planned to watch the man from a distance, at least figure out what he was up to. Instead, he stood less than a dozen feet away, bold as brass.

"What's wrong?"

Dane jerked his head toward the door, and at Destiny's audible gasp, knew she recognized the man in the charcoal-gray suit. Several other men stood surrounding him, all dressed like they'd come straight from a business meeting. As they walked past his table, Dane lowered his head slightly, not wanting the other man to get a good look at his face. He doubted MacKenna would recognize him, but he wasn't willing to take the chance. If he'd been the one to put the bounty on his head, then MacKenna would probably know what he looked like.

"Did you know he was going to be at this restaurant?"

"No, I swear. I knew he was in Vegas, but I had no clue we would end up at the same place at the same time."

Destiny simply shook her head, like she was disappointed in him for some reason. It hurt, because he was telling the truth. Well, mostly. He had planned to figure out a way to run into MacKenna, maybe see if there was a spark of recognition. From the few photos he'd been able to find, and from his memories, he knew he looked a lot like his biological father.

"Were you planning on telling me or was I going to be blindsided when I came face-to-face with the man who might have murdered your father?"

"Destiny—"

"I deserve better than this, Dane. I've done everything you've asked. I even told you there was a contract on your life. I researched, stuck my neck out, too. Shiloh might fire me for the stunt I've pulled, and for what? So you can cut me out of the loop and go rogue?"

"Can I talk now? It was not my intention to shut you out. Yes, I knew MacKenna was in Vegas. He's here working on a business takeover, another one of his many over the last ten years. Apparently, he's decided to try his hand at real estate. My source told me MacKenna thinks the market in Vegas is hot, one of the hottest in the country, and he's planning on acquiring one of the largest real estate firms in Nevada and turning it over to his son. Another arm for MacKenna-Duncan International."

"Lemme guess, you were going to barge into his meeting and confront him."

"Really? Do you think so little of me?"

She reached across the table and grabbed his hand. "I think you're running on emotion right now, and not intellect. You're thinking about getting up and going over to his table right now, aren't you?"

He gave a sheepish shrug because there was a part of him that wanted to do just that. It was a stupid move, he knew, but it would be satisfying to watch the older man grow pale, knowing that the one loose end he'd left dangling after murdering Dane's parents was alive—and looking for revenge.

"A knee jerk reaction will only get you in trouble. Or dead. How do you know the person who's trying to kill you isn't sitting at the table with MacKenna right now?"

"I don't."

"Exactly. Let's be smart about this. We're close to having the information you'll need to bring MacKenna down, financially and criminally. But if you jump the gun, it will backfire, I promise you. Not only will he walk away looking like the aggrieved party, but you'll look like the villain." She squeezed his hand, and Dane sighed, knowing she was right. He didn't like it, but she made sense.

"Fine. Let's finish our dinner and head back to the hotel. Maybe we can find out if there's another reason MacKenna is in Vegas."

Destiny smiled, and he knew she'd forgiven him. Something deep inside unfurled, a warmth spreading through him like sunshine on a summer day.

"You know, somehow I hadn't pictured spending my wedding night on the computer, looking for dirt to bring down a killer."

"Destiny—"

"Just kidding. Dane, lighten up. It's all part of why we're here, right? Getting married is simply a business arrangement. The sooner we find the evidence you need, the sooner we can get an annulment and things can go back to normal."

"It seems strange, we've been married for less than two hours and we're already talking about going our separate ways. Seems kind of, I don't know, weird."

As he spoke, Dane felt an itch between his shoulder blades, along with the overwhelming feeling of being watched. He stiffened imperceptibly, but obviously enough Destiny noticed. He watched as she scanned the restaurant, looking for any threat.

"See anything?"

She gave a brief shake of her head, then added, "Nothing obvious, but Matthew MacKenna keeps glancing at our table. Do you think he recognized you?"

"He would if he's the one who's been trying to find the missing Duncan boy. Somebody is. I've gotten alerts on several websites over the past three days."

"Me too. I meant to ask, do you have any idea why

somebody started looking for you in the first place?"

"They aren't looking for me. They are looking for Thomas Elliot Duncan. Missing son of Peter and Marjorie Duncan of Denver, Colorado. Nobody should know Thomas Duncan and Dane Boudreau are the same person, except for the person trying to find the six-year-old who disappeared the night his parents were killed."

Destiny surreptitiously reached for his cell phone and clicked on the camera app. Pretending to take a picture of him, she focused on the table behind him and over his shoulder. She quickly snapped several photos, then placed the cell back on the tabletop.

"Smart. Hopefully we can identify the other men at the table with MacKenna."

"I recognize one of them. His son, Owen."

Dane started to turn, wondering why he hadn't recognized Owen when he walked in. Destiny's hand on his arm stopped him. She shook her head and pointed to his cell phone.

"Don't turn around, it'll only draw attention. Look at the phone, like you're checking messages. Owen's the one in the Navy jacket, no tie. Top couple buttons are undone. Brown hair and brown eyes. Doesn't much resemble his father, at least in looks."

Glancing at his phone, Dane studied the photos Destiny had snapped. A man probably in his early forties sat beside MacKenna and instantly drew his focus. He vaguely remembered Owen MacKenna from when he was a kid. Owen had been about nine or ten years older than him. A memory of them playing hide-and-seek while their fathers worked in their home's study popped into his mind. He remembered Owen hadn't treated him like a nuisance or a brat, instead of spending time coloring and doing puzzles with a precocious six-year-old. The man seated beside Matthew MacKenna barely resembled the teenager who'd put up with him tagging along and constantly getting underfoot.

There was nothing relaxed or calm about this Owen. Though he'd removed his tie, he still exemplified the astute businessman, right down to his highly polished shoes. Dane intuitively knew Owen MacKenna wasn't a man he'd want to cross, at business or play. He'd be a ruthless, cutthroat opponent.

When the chef laid a couple of loaded plates in front of them, Dane glanced down at the steaming hot entree, realizing he'd missed most of the show, occupied with figuring out why Matthew MacKenna was here at the same restaurant he'd chosen to bring Destiny.

He'd meant for tonight to be special, a treat for Destiny. She'd played along with everything he'd asked, helping him uncover information on MacKenna and his associates. She hadn't once moaned or complained, even at his outlandish demand for marriage to protect his family. Instead of showing gratitude for her help, he'd let his obsession with his father's former partner cloud everything except his desire to bring the man to justice.

I'm an idiot.

"This isn't the evening I had planned, you know."

"Really? I'm not complaining."

"That's because you're a saint. And I'm a jackass. Let's try and forget about MacKenna, at least for tonight, and enjoy our meal. We can start fresh in the morning and look at things with clear heads. Deal?"

She studied his face, and whatever she saw must have convinced her, because she held out her hand. "Deal."

Wrapping his hand around hers, he felt the chill of her fingers, and reached for her other hand, and began rubbing them, warming them with his touch. She didn't resist, simply allowing him to hold her hands within his. Showing a level of trust he wasn't sure he'd earned—yet. But he would.

Reluctantly, he released them and picked up his chopsticks, and popped a whole shrimp in his mouth. He remembered one of his friends in school had introduced him to teppanyaki. Invited over for dinner, his friend's mom had prepared a Japanese feast. Dane had been fascinated, watching her quick and assured movements with the knives and hot template. Throughout dinner, she'd taught him the proper way of eating a teppanyaki meal, including putting your chopsticks down between bites, and never to point with your chopsticks. It's considered impolite.

"So, Mrs. Boudreau, how does it feel to be a married

woman?"

He watched color flood her cheeks turning them a delightful pink, and his grin grew wider. The chunky shortcut of her deep brown hair curved around her face, and he couldn't help thinking how beautiful she looked in the filtered light of the restaurant. The warm glow couldn't hide the startling blue of her eyes, or her full, kissable lips.

The kiss at their wedding, he hadn't planned it. All he'd contemplated was a brush of his lips against her cheek. But when the minister said the words he could kiss his bride, he'd wanted—no, he'd needed—to kiss her. To feel what her mouth felt like beneath his. He'd caught her gasp when he'd parted her lips with his, yet he couldn't have stopped himself if the roof had crashed atop his head. Hunger drove his need, and all he could think about was wanting, needing, to kiss her again. And again.

"Well, so far, Mr. Boudreau, I can't complain."

"I hope we get a chance to see a few of the things Vegas is famous for before we head home. Maybe catch a show."

She ducked her head, hiding her gaze, and he wondered what she was thinking. Was she filled with regret for helping him? He'd asked a lot from someone who was basically a stranger, yet she hadn't balked or complained. It wasn't because she was a pushover, either. He knew from talking to Ridge and Shiloh that Destiny gave as good as she got. She didn't have a problem standing up to them when she thought they were being jerks. So why was she willing to put aside her life, her career, to help him?

"That's not why we're here, Dane. We came to get married—which we've done. Finding Matthew and Owen MacKenna here presents a unique opportunity, one we should seize if we get the chance."

"I know. I wish…" He trailed off, because what was the use of wishing for the unattainable. He couldn't bring somebody else into his mess. Couldn't think about sharing a life with anybody, not until he got justice for his parents.

"Don't. Today we took a major step toward protecting the legacy your father established. Let's enjoy our meal and worry about our next step in the morning." She lifted her glass and met his gaze. "To justice.

"To justice."

CHAPTER NINE

DESTINY SLID THE keycard into the lock, and turned the handle, pushing the door open slightly. She turned to Dane, who stood behind her. The whole evening, heck, the entire day, was mostly a blur. Except for the kiss at the end of the wedding ceremony. *That* was imprinted in her mind. There wasn't a chance she'd ever forget it.

"Good night, Dane. Thank you for dinner."

"Sorry it didn't turn out the way I'd hoped. It was supposed to be a thank you for helping me. Instead, I acted like a jerk and let my obsession with MacKenna ruin everything."

"Nothing was ruined. I'll always remember tonight."

Acting on impulse, she stood on her tiptoes and brushed a kiss against his cheek. It was a stupid thing to do, but she only had one wedding night, and if this was going to be it, she wanted to at least kiss her husband good night.

Pushing the door all the way open, she froze at the carnage that met her gaze. Everything was strewn all over. Her clothes littered the floor. The bedding was pulled from the mattress, hanging from one corner in a jumbled heap. The bedside lamp was toppled over, the shade dented. The drawers in the nightstand and the dresser were pulled out, emptied of everything they'd contained.

"Dane! My computer!"

She raced into the room, and he grabbed her arm, pulling her to a halt. "Wait. Let me make sure nobody's still here."

Drawing in a ragged breath, she nodded, her arms wrapped across her chest. Who'd done this? She didn't have any enemies, at least none in Las Vegas.

"Doesn't look like anybody's here. Come on in."

Her eyes couldn't seem to light on any single thing, moving from one thing to the next, unable to process what happened. Heading for the closet, she looked at the safe that came with the room. She hadn't wanted to leave her laptop out. There was too much sensitive information on it. Everything was backed up, so it wasn't like she didn't have access to all the information, and other laptops at home, but this one—it was her baby.

Entering the combination, she let out the breath she hadn't realized she was holding when she spotted the silver and black laptop. Ragged around the edges, and worn from use, it didn't appear to be worth more than a couple bucks, but the information it contained could prove to be priceless to Dane.

"I'm calling the front desk and have them notify security. You can't stay here tonight."

"I'm sure they'll give me another room."

"You're staying with me." There was a don't-argue-with-me tone in his voice. She was too tired to fight with him anyway. She simply nodded.

"Who would do this?"

"My guess? MacKenna's had somebody following us, probably since we left Shiloh Springs. This proves he's guilty. Nobody else has a reason."

A horrible thought had her reaching for his hand. "Do you think they did this to your room too?"

His eyes widened at her words, and he grabbed her laptop in one hand and pulled her behind him with the other. Since his room was right across the hall, he had the door open within seconds. Its interior was a match for her room. Everything had been tossed, scattered without care. They'd been looking for something.

"Did you leave anything here they might have taken?" She took in the devastation wrought by the intruders. It was almost a carbon copy of hers, right down to the stripped bed and knocked over lamps. It took a twisted kind of desperation to do something like this, especially in a place like the Bellagio. Backing out into the hallway, her eyes scanned its length and spotted what she was looking for.

Security cameras.

Dane's conversation with the front desk was curt and to the point. The scowl on his face betrayed his barely banked anger. Though it wasn't directed at her, Destiny pitied whoever ended up on the wrong side of this particular

Boudreau. Shiloh had mentioned once in passing that Dane was slow to anger, but once he reached his boiling point, the explosion of his temper could be felt for days.

"Security coming?"

He gave a jerking nod, bending to pick up a shirt off the floor. Giving a sigh of disgust, he dropped it back down again.

"They did a pretty thorough job of destroying everything. Luckily, I had the front desk store my computer in their safe. I don't trust the ones in the rooms."

Holding up her laptop, she quirked her brow. When he barked out a laugh, she felt the muscles bunched in the back of her neck begin to unwind.

"Point taken. The concierge is arranging for a suite for the rest of our stay. As soon as we're finished with security, it will be ready."

A noise from outside proved security had made a beeline for their rooms, and Destiny followed Dane out into the hall. She watched the workers going through their rooms, while Dane spoke quietly with the head of security. Within a few minutes, they got the all-clear to begin gathering their things.

By the time they finished, the concierge stood outside Dane's room, apologizing profusely.

"I'm sorry, Mr. Boudreau. We have contacted the Las Vegas Police Department, and they are sending officers right over. As we discussed, I've arranged a deluxe suite to be put at your disposal for the remainder of your stay. On the house, of course. Anything you need, simply let me or the front desk know, and we'll do our best to accommodate your needs. Again, I apologize for this unforeseen incident." He handed Dane two keycards.

"I spoke with your head of security and asked to see the security footage of this floor." Dane's casual demeanor, his forced smile, sent a shiver down Destiny's spine. She hoped he never turned that look on her because she'd melt like chocolate in summer.

"Yes, he's already spoken to me, and I've authorized him to show you the footage for this evening. Will there be anything else, Mr. Boudreau?" He turned and smiled at Destiny. "Ms. Smith, if there's anything you need…"

"I'm fine." She patted her laptop. "I've got what I need, right here."

"Excellent. I hope this doesn't ruin your evening." He turned to go, and Dane chimed in.

"You mean our wedding night."

The concierge visibly paled at the bald statement. "I'm sorry, did you say it's your wedding night?"

"We were married earlier this evening. Came back from our celebration dinner to this." Dane swept his hand toward the open door of his room.

"I'll have champagne delivered to your new suite immediately, sir. Congratulations on your marriage. May it be long and joyful."

Destiny watched as the poor man practically sprinted toward the elevator, almost stumbling in his haste to get away from Dane. She shook his head, giving Dane a chastising look.

"You could have given the guy a break. He couldn't have known we just got married. Probably wouldn't have occurred to him, anyway, since we were staying in separate rooms."

"If anybody comes nosing around, asking about us, I want them to hear we're on our honeymoon. MacKenna can't accuse me of stalking him if I've got a bona fide reason for being in Las Vegas. Namely my beautiful bride."

"Please, Dane, drop the act. Nobody's around and I don't need insincere flattery. I'm already committed to getting the job done. I'm not going to back out."

Dane took a step closer, and placed a fingertip beneath her chin, tilting it up. "I don't say things I don't mean, princess. You are beautiful. You are honest, sincere, and genuinely care about people. You proved that when you went out on a limb to call me when you discovered someone was out to hurt me. That shows a beauty of character that few people possess."

Tears pricked her eyelids, and she blinked fast to hold them back. His words rang with sincerity, not false flattery. Even in the midst of dealing with break-ins, shuffling rooms, and looking for a killer, he still took time to think about her feelings. She needed to put a tight rein on them feelings because if she didn't keep her guard up, she'd end up falling hard for her cowboy.

"Thank you."

His hand reached up and cupped her cheek, his thumb brushing lightly against her skin, and her eyelids drifted shut, feeling a tingle at his simple touch. She opened her mouth, not sure what she'd say, when his hand dropped. Instantly, she missed his touch.

"We should probably head up to our new room."

"You're right. Nothing's being accomplished standing here in the hall. Did you want to go down and get your computer?"

He shook his head. "Not tonight. I'll deal with it in the morning. Let's get settled in. It's been a long day."

Without another word, he spun and headed for the elevator. Breathing out a deep sigh, Destiny followed.

"WHO CAME UP with the bright idea to trash Boudreau's room?"

Owen MacKenna spun around at his father's angry question. Relaxing his hands from the clenched fists they'd curled into, he watched the old man pace in front of the bank of windows in their suite. He hadn't planned on coming on this fool's errand with his father. The old man could have done this takeover in his sleep. After all, he'd been doing them for decades. He should be home, figuring out a solution to their

Boudreau problem, because it looked like it was about to bite them in the backside.

"Wasn't me. When did this happen?"

"One of my sources informed me Dane Boudreau's hotel room at the Bellagio was ransacked, as well as the room of his traveling companion."

Owen tapped his fingers on the desk where he was seated. He'd been on his computer, putting out a few fires back home, when his father had burst into the room, flinging accusations.

"Lovely woman, if she's the one he was dining with tonight. Do we know who she is?"

"Somebody named Destiny Smith. Although as of a few hours ago, she's now Destiny Boudreau."

Owen chuckled, the sound low and deep. He doubted his father got his sarcastic wit. "Lucky guy."

"Are you insane? Having a wife could ruin everything."

"Still doesn't answer the question of who trashed their rooms. If I didn't do it, and you say you didn't do it, any guesses who might want to rattle Dane's cage?"

His father spun toward him, his face a fiery red. If he wasn't careful, he'd end up with a heart attack. At his last checkup, the doctor told him to take it easy, because his blood pressure was dangerously high. He couldn't afford for the old goat to croak. Not yet. There were still a few threads knotted that needed unraveling before that could happen.

"This is not a joke, you idiot! You know who Dane Boudreau is—we have the DNA report to prove it. If he's uncovered what happened in Denver, he can take everything away. Everything we've spent years building. We can't let that happen."

Owen stood and walked over to place a hand on his father's shoulder. "Calm down, old man. My sources say Dane Boudreau doesn't have a clue who he really is. He's digging, but there's no paper trail for him to find. Nothing online, either. No matter how deep he goes, we've covered our tracks too well. Even if he somehow figures out he's Thomas Duncan, it will take years, maybe decades before he can do anything about taking the company from you."

"He knows. One look into his eyes tonight at the restaurant and I'm sure. He knows everything rightfully belongs to him, and he's coming after us."

Owen barely resisted the urge to wrap his hands around his father's neck and squeeze and squeeze as he watched the life fade from his eyes. How he hated his father. Hated him for every wrong turn in his life. Every decision that backfired. Every time, he'd had to bow and scrape for his father's approval, yet never getting it.

"Let him try. He's got nothing and you know it. There's nothing online anywhere that connects you with his parents outside of business. MacKenna-Duncan International is a thriving business that Thomas Elliot Duncan contributed nothing to, and he won't see one red cent. Besides, everybody knows Thomas was declared legally dead years ago."

Matthew walked over to the bar, and poured a stiff shot of whiskey, knocking it back in a single gulp. Owen simply shook his head. His father had been depending on alcohol increasingly the last few years. A guilty conscience maybe, from too many years of plundering away peoples' lives, their companies, with the snap of his fingers. Let him wallow in his misery. He deserved it.

"Put Evans on it. Have him find out who trashed the two rooms at the Bellagio. We don't need to give Boudreau any ammunition to come after us, especially for something we didn't do." Matthew slammed his fist against the desk.

"Calm down. If Boudreau knows anything, we'll handle him." Owen poured himself a drink, taking a small sip. Admitting to his father that he'd ordered the rooms searched, hoping to find out exactly how much Dane Boudreau really knew was out of the question. His dad's grip had become tenuous in the last years, and if he thought Owen made decisions and took action without consulting him, it might push him over the edge.

"We can't lose everything now, son. We've worked too hard for too long to have it slip through our fingers." His father collapsed onto the corner of the bed and hung his head in his hands. "I did this all for you."

Owen let out a low sigh, before handing his glass to his father. "I know, Dad. I know."

CHAPTER TEN

D ANE ROLLED OVER and glanced at the clock on the nightstand. It was barely six in the morning, and he had less than two hours sleep. With the move to the new suite, and making sure Destiny got settled into her bedroom, he'd tossed and turned most of the night. He couldn't get Matthew MacKenna out of his head.

He couldn't make heads or tails of why their rooms had been trashed. Did MacKenna think he was stupid enough to leave anything lying around that might clue him in to what evidence Dane had accumulated? He might not have any specialized skills with law enforcement, other than what his brothers taught him, but he also wasn't a rube who just fell off the turnip truck.

Besides, everything he had fed directly to a secure server, encoded and password protected, as well as hard copies which he'd given to an attorney for safekeeping, which would be forwarded to the FBI as well as distributed to every major newspaper in the country. He'd also made certain that Antonio and Lucas got copies because they'd make sure the facts didn't get buried under a pile of hush money.

Whispers of memory floated through his thoughts, of a young woman, just getting started on her life. Working her way through college, she'd taken on the part-time tutor/babysitter gig for a six-year-old, never realizing that single decision would alter her life forever. As a boy, he liked Ginger. She was fun. She didn't mind when he got loud or wanted to play for hours. Patiently teaching him, telling him stories, and watching all his favorite animated movies.

She hadn't deserved to die.

A hard pounding on the hotel's door had him jumping up from the bed, instantly alert. Blood pumped through his veins, spiked with a rush of adrenaline until he realized the bad guys usually didn't knock loud enough to wake other guests. He stalked to the door and flung it open.

"What?"

He stumbled back when a hand shoved against his chest—hard. Three tall, broad-shouldered men pushed past him, almost overpowering the space. With an exaggerated eye roll, Dane closed the door and leaned against it, staring at his brothers.

"Wakey-wakey, sunshine. You've got some explaining to do." Antonio's smirk made Dane want to wipe it off his face, with his fist. Couldn't do that. Momma frowned upon them fighting—no matter how much they deserved a good beating.

"Don't know what you're talking about."

Shiloh simply walked to the phone and started placing a

breakfast order, requesting lots of hot coffee. The amount of food he ordered was enough to feed a dozen people, not just the four of them. No, make that five when he counted Destiny. His eyes strayed toward the closed bedroom door, praying she didn't wake up. Maybe he could get his brothers out of here before they realized Destiny was in his suite.

Too late.

The door opened and Destiny stood silhouetted in the light flooding through the open drapes. He hadn't bothered closing them the night before, opting instead to watch the waters from the fountain. The light coming through diffused around her like a halo, and she had that mussed, just got out of bed look that made him want to rush his brothers out the door and make love to her. She was his wife after all, even if he'd spent a long, lonely night alone in his bed.

"Told you. Pay up, bro."

Heath reached into his wallet and pulled out a twenty. "I hate it when you're right."

"Right about what?" Destiny walked over to stand by Dane, and he slid his arm around her waist.

"I bet him that you were with our brother. What I don't know is why?" Shiloh's gaze narrowed, immediately taking in the intimate picture Dane knew he saw. Destiny, dressed in a long T-shirt, her legs bare. Fortunately, the oversized shirt hit her below mid-thigh, or he might have to punch his brother in the face. Didn't hurt that Shiloh had already found the love of his life and wasn't about to stray. Same with Heath and Antonio, though they did seem curious about why she was with Dane.

"The better question is, what are you three bozos doing here?"

"Looking for you. First, Destiny takes off with pretty much no notice, saying she needs some personal time. Okay, I can buy that, though she's never missed a day of work since I hired her." When she started to speak, Shiloh held up his hand, stopping her. "Then you have Dom take over running the ranch while you go 'out of town for a few days.'" His exact words. He clammed up good and tight after that, refusing to give us any answers. Just so you know, Dad's sticking around the ranch for a few days, just in case."

"Still doesn't explain why you're here." Dane decided if they were going to do this, he might as well get comfortable. His brothers were here, and there was no way they weren't going to get answers. Especially Antonio. He'd burrow deep like a tick, and not turn loose until he found out everything he needed to know.

Keeping his arm around Destiny's waist, he led her into the living room and sat beside her on the couch.

"Good idea. Might as well get comfy. Room service said it might take a while."

"You ordered room service? Hope you told them to send extra coffee." Destiny's words were broken by a huge yawn and Dane smiled. She looked cute, with her hair tousled from sleep and, without any makeup. He especially liked how she leaned against his side, while his brothers sat on the sofa across from them.

"It's a long story."

"Bro, I kind of figured that much out when you high-tailed it to Vegas. Now, what kind of business could you possibly have here?" Shiloh's voice had gone from joking and friendly to deadly serious from one heartbeat to the next.

"For somebody who's supposed to be the smart one, you sure aren't very observant." Heath managed to reach past Antonio's shoulder and popped Shiloh in the back of the head. "Look at their left hands, dummy."

Destiny held up her left hand, flashing the gold and diamond band Dane had put on her finger less than twenty-four hours prior. He wore a matching plain gold band on his ring finger. Shiloh choked on his gasp, and Antonio pounded his back, before turning a grin toward Dane.

"Congratulations, bro."

"Thanks." Sliding his arm around Destiny's shoulder, he leaned in and rubbed his cheek against the top of her head. She seemed to get the message, because she cuddled closer against his side, looking like a loving bride.

"Hang on a second." Shiloh shifted his gaze between Dane and Destiny, before zeroing in on her. He pointed an accusatory finger at her. "You barely know my brother. You've met him what, a handful of times. And now you're married?"

"We've spent a lot of time talking. Texting and messaging. Getting to know each other. I know it's fast, but when it's the right person, it feels right, and you just—you know they're the one. Isn't that how it happened with you and Maggie?"

"Not the same thing, Destiny. I was around her a lot more than you've been around Dane. Maggie and I were living under the same roof, and—"

"I'm not buying it." Heath leaned forward, the muscles beneath his leather jacket rippled with his movements. "Part of my job is being able to tell when somebody's lying, little brother. And while you're not outright lying, you sure aren't telling the whole truth."

Dane turned to look at Destiny. "I hate it when he calls me that. He's four months older than me. Four months, and he's gotta lord it over me like he's the big bad."

Heath turned toward Antonio and Shiloh. "See how he's deflecting and trying to change the subject? Typical of somebody who's either hiding something, or he's a big ole liar."

Dane waved his middle finger at his brother, who simply grinned.

"You don't want to play nice, bro? Well, how about we start this conversation again?" Shiloh leaned back and stretched his arm along the back of the sofa. "Why are you in Vegas? Besides marrying my favorite computer expert, that is. We'll definitely be talking about that later, Destiny, but right now I want the truth. Are you in some kind of trouble?" His eyes widened. "Please, please tell me you're not pregnant."

"I'm not pregnant."

Dane pulled in a deep breath and let it out slowly. He was busted and he knew it. They'd have learned the truth eventually, but he'd wanted to tell Momma and Dad first. Too late now; his brothers weren't about to leave without a good explanation. Especially if they caught a whiff of something that might affect the family. One thing about a Boudreau, they protected their own.

"Dane, you should tell them. Maybe they can help."

"Yeah, what she said." Heath stood at the knock on the door. "But don't say anything until I get back."

Room service unloaded the mountain of food and two carafes of coffee onto the table between the two couches and left, smiling at the large tip Heath slid into his hand. Almost immediately, Antonio grabbed a plate, loaded it with scrambled eggs and sausage, and began slathering a bagel with cream cheese. Shrugging, Dane handed a matching plate to his bride and began pouring coffee. After passing one to Destiny, who smiled, he took his own plate and leaned back, sipping his orange juice.

"You can talk and eat at the same time, Dane."

"Sheesh, give a guy a break. I'm starving."

"If we have to ask one more time, I'm calling Momma. We didn't tell her you'd hightailed it to Las Vegas. How do you think she's gonna take it when she finds out about you and Destiny? She's going to be heartbroken you eloped without a word." Heath's shark-like grin had Dane hanging his head. He felt guilty enough having finagled Destiny into what practically amounted to a shotgun wedding, minus the shotgun, but nobody could make him feel like a schoolboy caught with his hand in the cookie jar than his mother. Man, if she cried, he was doomed.

"Fine. You guys remember when I came to live at the Big House?" At their nods, he continued. "Nobody knew anything about who I was. Where I came from. I didn't talk, hadn't spoken since I'd been picked up by Child Protective Services."

"I remember." Antonio shot him a sympathetic look. "You were pretty much a ghost. Physically there, but almost like you wanted to be invisible."

"I'd been living with a young woman named Ginger. She'd been my tutor and babysitter. She was my best friend, and I got her killed."

The bite Antonio was about to take froze halfway to his mouth before he lowered the fork to his plate. "What?"

"It goes back to about six weeks before I went into CPS. Ginger took care of me, especially when my parents had to go to business stuff. Dinner parties, meetings, that kind of thing."

"Wait a second. I thought you couldn't remember anything about your life before you came to live with us." Shiloh leaned forward, staring at Dane. "I remember how much that bothered Momma. She hated that you didn't have any memories about who you were, where you came from."

Dane sighed. "That was a lie. I never told anybody, because I was scared. Terrified that whoever killed my parents, killed Ginger, would find me and kill me, too."

Stunned silence met his bald statement. He could see the wheels turning in his brothers' heads, as they processed his words.

"Your parents were murdered? How do you remember that?" Antonio was the first to ask, which made sense. He processed information quickly, his analytical brain already switching into his FBI persona.

"I've always known. We—Ginger and I—were in the house when they were murdered. They'd just gotten home, barely made it through the front door. I remember hearing a noise and a scream. Ginger told me to hush, and she tiptoed to the top of the staircase. When she came back, she picked me up and started running down the back stairs. I remember she was crying and shaking. She made me get down on the floorboards behind the driver's seat. I didn't know about my parents, but I knew something bad happened because we weren't supposed to leave the house—ever—when my folks weren't home."

Destiny sat her plate on the table, and took his hand, threading her fingers through his, and leaned her head against his shoulder. Her simple touch offered silent comfort, giving him a peaceful calm to continue.

"It wasn't until a couple of days later when she told me my parents weren't ever coming back. I didn't know what dead meant, and she was so young she'd probably never dealt with somebody she knew dying, either. But she was smart. Smart enough to know she couldn't trust anybody."

"Couldn't she have called the cops?"

"Good question, Heath. But I'm more interested in who Dane's parents were, because it sounds like that's a big part of his story." Antonio's sympathetic gaze nearly undid him, but Dane knew he needed to keep going. Get the story out, because his family deserved justice, and he was determined to make sure they got it.

While Dane had been talking, Shiloh had been working feverishly on his phone, and when he looked up and met his eyes, Dane knew he'd figured it out. At least the who part of the equation.

"Denver, right?" Dane nodded, the knot in his throat now too big to speak around. "Twenty-five years ago?"

"Yeah."

Shiloh handed his phone to Antonio, who quickly scanned whatever was on the screen before handing the phone to Heath. He watched his brother's eyes grow rounder as he realized the enormity of what he was seeing.

"Peter and Marjorie Duncan? Murdered in a home invasion robbery. Their only son went missing on the night of the murders and was never found."

"That's right."

"Dane, that means you're—"

"I'm Thomas Elliot Duncan, and I'm going to make the man who killed my parents pay."

CHAPTER ELEVEN

DESTINY SAT ON the high stool in front of a slot machine, and pushed the button, not paying attention to the whirling sounds or the tumblers. No, her eyes were glued to Owen MacKenna, seated several feet away at a blackjack table. Dane and his brothers were off somewhere, putting their heads together and making plans to confront Matthew MacKenna with the fact Dane was the missing Duncan heir, Thomas Elliot Duncan.

Honestly, she thought they were making a mistake, tipping their hand this early in the game. While the mountain of evidence she and Dane collected was overwhelming, it wasn't a given it would hold up in a court of law. She knew for Dane it wasn't about the money. Financial gain didn't have anything to do with his reason for wanting to bring down Matthew MacKenna. He wanted justice. He wanted to avenge his parents' murder. He wanted—peace.

Pushing the button again, she watched Owen hand a high-dollar chip to the dealer and stand. Dang it, he was leaving. Bells and sirens blared, the sounds shrill and far too close. She jumped, realizing it was her machine making the racket. She'd won. Not a gigantic jackpot, but still a couple hundred dollars. Who'd have thought she'd hit right when Owen decided to leave?

Grabbing the voucher for her winnings, she shoved it in her pocket and stood, following Owen through the archway of the casino and toward the bar area. She wrinkled her nose at the overwhelming stench from cigarette smoke. Ugh, she hated smoking. Her mom had smoked while Destiny was growing up, and she'd hated it. Hated the smell and the taste and the fact that her mother couldn't quit. It was the one thing about her mom she'd had a problem with, because not only did it make the house unbearable, but more than once her mother had gotten in trouble at work because she got caught smoking when she shouldn't. Now she was going to have to burn these clothes because she'd never get the smell out, and she certainly didn't want to pack them into her bag to take back home.

When Owen walked through the door to the bar, she knew she'd guessed right. He'd been losing consistently, ever since she spotted him at the blackjack table. Maybe he planned on drowning his bad luck in booze. Slipping through the opening, she looked around. While the place was crowded, they weren't packed in like sardines, so she was able to breathe.

Owen took a seat at the bar, and she knew she had a decision to make. The wrong move could blow everything. Yet, how often did an opportunity like this come up? She doubted he'd noticed her that night in the Japanese restaurant. Nobody would associate her with Dane. Still, it was a risk.

Taking a deep breath, she pulled back her shoulders and stood tall. She headed toward the bar and slid onto a stool one seat away from Owen. When the bartender asked for her order, she picked a soda. She'd learned a long time ago she and alcohol weren't a good combination. It had been almost ten years since she'd touched the stuff and had no plans on changing that tonight.

Owen lifted his glass, and she watched the golden whiskey disappear down his throat. He motioned for another.

"Run of bad luck?"

His head swiveled in her direction at her question, and she studied him, looking for signs of recognition. Nothing flared in his eyes, except maybe a flicker of interest when his eyes strayed to her boobs. Great, not only was Owen MacKenna a lush, but he was also a loser. This was a bad idea, but it was too late to back out now.

"It was until now. Can I buy you a drink? Maybe something a little stronger than that?" He gestured toward her soda.

"Thanks, but I'm good with this. Appreciate the offer, though. As a matter of fact, how about I buy you another one? I've done pretty well tonight."

Lifting his glass, he downed what was in his glass in one gulp. "Sure, why not?"

Motioning to the bartender, she indicated Owen's glass and held up one finger. At his nod, she turned her attention back to Owen. This was the first time she'd had a chance to study the man, other than in photographs. She knew the basic facts. He was forty-two, ten years older than Dane. Married once and divorced after three years. He maintained a gym membership and kept himself in decent physical shape, though if he kept hitting the bottle like he was tonight, that wouldn't last.

"You in Vegas for business or pleasure?"

"A little of both. I'm babysitting my dad, making sure he doesn't do anything to get in over his head. How about you?"

Making sure he wasn't looking, she slid her wedding ring off, saying a silent *sorry* to Dane. "I'm here to have some fun. I work hard and I like to play hard. I haven't had a break all year and decided after my last job I needed to take a step back and relax."

"Now that's a sentiment I can understand. I've been focused on nothing but business for the last couple of years, Nothing but work, work, work. Sounds like we're kindred spirits."

This time he took a smaller sip of his drink, and she wondered if he'd loosen up more if she got him someplace a little quieter. It couldn't hurt to try, right?

"If you don't have plans, would you like to maybe have dinner with me?" She gave a simpering giggle and wanted to vomit. This wasn't her. She wasn't the girl who flirted with guys. Heck, she didn't even know how to flirt.

He gave her another assessing look, before answering. Convinced he was going to turn her down, she started to rise.

"You know what? I don't have anything pending that can't wait. I'd love to have dinner with you." He tossed back the remainder of his drink and rose.

"Awesome. Give me just one minute, I need to call my friend and tell her I've made other plans." She waggled her cell phone, knowing she needed to let Dane know she wouldn't be back for a while. Chances were good he hadn't even noticed she'd left the suite.

"Go ahead. I'll check my messages, and then we'll head out."

Turning in her chair, she dialed Dane's number.

"Where are you? I went to check and see if you wanted to go out for dinner, and you were gone."

"Oh, hi, Nica. Listen, we're going to have to change our plans. I'm going out to dinner with a...friend, um," she glanced at Owen and whispered, "what's your name?"

With a smile, he answered. "Owen. Owen MacKenna."

"I'm going to dinner with a new friend, Owen MacKenna. I'll be back later."

Dane's voice raised in shock, "Destiny what do you think you're doing? Where are you? I'll come—"

"There's nothing to worry about, Nica. It's just dinner,

here at the hotel." She mouthed, "Is that okay?" to Owen, who nodded.

"Princess, don't you dare go with him. He knows who you are, and—"

"No, it's okay, we'll catch up later, I promise. Don't wait up."

She hung up at the sound of Dane's sputtered yell. Oh, she was going to hear about it when she got back to their room, but this was too good an opportunity to pass up.

"You ready to go?" Owen extended his arm, and she slid her hand through the crook of his elbow. She gave him a flirty smile.

"Absolutely."

It didn't take more than a few minutes to walk through the doors of the steakhouse. Owen slid several bills into the hostess' hand, and before she could blink, they were led to a private table beside large windows next to the water. Owen pulled her chair out, before taking the one across from her. The setting was intimate, warm, and cozy, with the illusion they were alone in the midst of a large restaurant. She liked the whole vibe of the place and wished she was there with Dane.

"This is a beautiful place. Have you been here before?" She picked up her napkin with a gentle flick of her wrist and placed it on her lap. Within seconds, a waiter arrived to take their drink order. He looked surprised when she again ordered a soda and surprised her again when he got the same.

"Tell me about yourself, sweetheart. How'd you end up in Sin City?"

"Well, I work in IT. Mostly data input, boring but it pays well. My friend, Nica—the one I called earlier—we've been putting in a ton of info recently, because of a corporate merger. Some kind of buyout by corporate bigwigs. I don't pay a lot of attention to that kind of thing, you know? As long as my paycheck clears, and I've got enough money to have a little fun, I'm good."

She hoped Nica didn't mind Destiny using her name in vain. But calling Dane by his sister's name would have clued him she was working an angle. Of course, she'd probably get her back side handed to her when she got back to the room. Dane wouldn't appreciate being left out of the loop, and he really wouldn't like her going out on her own, especially with a MacKenna.

He took a sip of his drink, studying her closely. When they'd been in the bar earlier, he hadn't shown any sign of recognition, and she hoped the drinks he had earlier kept him from recognizing her. "Funny, my company does that. Buys other companies, incorporating them into our business. Small world."

"Wow, maybe I'm working for you. Wouldn't that be funny?" She ran her hand through her short hair, wishing it was long and flowing because all the sexy women did that weird hair flipping thing when they were flirting. All she had going for her was her cleavage, which Owen kept staring at.

Trying not to be obvious, she surreptitiously tugged her top down a smidge lower, exposing the edge of her tattoo.

Let's see how you like this, Mr. Sleazebag.

A blooming rose in shades of crimson and lighter red, the petals looked like velvet, realistic and lifelike. The realism the artist achieved looked like a photograph, a flower just been plucked from a garden. On the flower a seated fairy kicked her legs, her wings half-furled behind her. Long dark hair spilled across the fairy's shoulders and onto a sapphire blue dress covering her ethereal body. While the scene appeared whimsical, the artist's ability made the scene come alive. A single dewdrop glistened on a rose petal, appearing to hang from its edge. She had other tattoos, but this one was her favorite.

"Let's not talk about business tonight. Instead, let's make a toast." Owen lifted his glass. "To finding new friends in the most unexpected places."

She touched her glass to his and took a small sip. A chill skittered down her spine at the sensation she was being watched. Trying not to be obvious, she looked around the restaurant, but she couldn't see anybody who seemed to be paying attention to her or Owen. It had to be her overactive imagination. She'd understand if she was out with Dane, because she knew somebody was watching him. Stalking him. And she'd made it her job to keep him safe—no matter what.

When the waiter came, she ordered a small filet and a

side salad. Owen ordered the porterhouse and a baked potato. Typical meat and potatoes for the man, she mused.

Owen was charming, kept the conversation moving, clearly at home with small talk without giving out any important details. Heck, they might as well be talking about the weather. At this rate, she wasn't going to find out anything useful and would've wasted her evening. She might as well have stayed in the room doing research; it would have been more productive.

Before she knew it, dinner was finished, and the plates cleared away. Steaming cups of coffee appeared as if by magic, the perfect kind of service. She made a mental note to leave a generous tip.

"It's still early, much too soon to call it a night. Would you like to explore a bit of Las Vegas with me?"

Taken aback by his proposal, Destiny scrambled to come up with a legitimate excuse, coming up blank.

"What do you have in mind? Remember, I promised Nica I'd be back after dinner."

"I thought maybe we could walk down the strip for a bit, look at the lights. There's nothing else like it anywhere. You said we need a break from work, something to take our minds off everything. A little stroll, some sightseeing, and pleasant conversation. Please say yes."

What could she say that wouldn't raise his suspicions? "Sure, sounds fun."

"Excellent." He motioned to their server, who immediately presented the bill to Owen. He signed it, charging it to his room. Some detective she was; she hadn't even realized he was staying in the same hotel as her and Dane.

"I was supposed to be taking you to dinner, remember?"

He smiled and held out his hand. "You can pick up the check next time."

He thinks there's going to be a next time? Is this dude delusional?

Exiting the hotel, they headed toward the bright lights. Destiny had to admit, she was impressed with the overall grandeur and excess of the city's famous landmarks. She imagined Sin City in its heyday, with the world-famous casinos and hotels sprawling from one end to the other, all festooned with neon lights. It hosted the best of the best in entertainment, both then and now. Extravaganzas featuring showgirls, strutting their stuff across the stages with feathered headdresses and barely-there skimpy outfits. It was too bad all of that faded glory ended before she was born.

If they weren't here on business, she'd make Dane take her to one of the shows, just so she could say she'd experienced an honest-to-goodness Vegas spectacular.

Crowds of people bustled around, laughing and having fun, and Destiny found herself relaxing as she walked beside Owen. He pointed out different sites to her. Stopping in front of The Mirage, she noted a crowd beginning to form.

"What's going on?"

"The Mirage volcano eruption show will be starting in

about twenty minutes. Attracts a lot of tourists."

"I'd forgotten about that. Doesn't it have lights and music synced to the explosions?"

Owen grinned. "That's what they told me. I made a reservation earlier, planned on popping over here if I finished up. Before running into you, my night was a real bummer, but things have certainly picked up. Would you like to watch the show with me?

"It's pretty crowded, I'm not sure we'll be able to see much from back here." She gestured toward the crowd, which was growing bigger by the minute.

"We'll have a much better view from the valet station. A friend told me it's one of the best places, we'll have unobstructed views of the whole show. You game?"

"Absolutely!" She didn't have to fake her excitement, because this was a once in a lifetime experience she didn't want to miss.

Within minutes they were standing at the valet kiosk, with a group of people, close to the wall, and with a fantastic view of the whole show. The whole music and fireworks spectacular lasted about five minutes, but it was worth the wait. Destiny was almost sorry when it ended, but when she caught a glimpse of the time and winced. If she didn't get back to the hotel soon, Dane would call out the cavalry, i.e., his brothers, and they'd mount a search.

"I've enjoyed tonight, but it's time I get back to the hotel. I've got a lot going on tomorrow, and I've got to get up early."

Owen studied her face before finally shrugging. "If that's what you want."

Walking side-by-side, they threaded their way through the crowd. Most people looked like they were just starting their evening, full of energy and cheerful spirits. She, on the other hand, felt like she could barely put one foot in front of the other.

The cool night air revived her a little, but it also made a shiver run through her. Owen pulled off his jacket and draped it over her shoulders, and she wondered again how someone who acted like a gentleman in public could protect a man like his father. She was convinced Dane was right, and Matthew MacKenna bore the responsibility for Dane's biological parents' deaths.

Waiting at the corner for the streetlight to change so they could cross, Destiny watched Owen pull his phone out and check a message. He obviously wasn't happy with whatever he read, because he frowned before shoving the phone back in his pocket.

The light changed, and she took a step off the curb, suddenly anxious to get back to the hotel, and Dane. The night had pretty well been a bust. While dinner was pleasant, Owen hadn't revealed anything they didn't already know. They weren't any closer to figuring out who'd put the hit on Dane or having the evidence to put Matthew MacKenna away for murder.

She'd barely taken two steps when she heard the squeal of brakes and felt a hard thump on her side. Excruciating pain blossomed in her hip. Strong arms wrapped around her before she hit the asphalt, pulling her back onto the sidewalk as people milled around. Loud voices bombarded her, and someone asked if she wanted to call the police.

"Are you alright? You got hit pretty hard." Owen's voice rose above the crowd, and she focused on him. Throbbing pain in her hip had her biting her lip, and she drew in a ragged breath before answering.

"I'm fine. A little banged up, but none the worse for wear. Where'd that car come from? I looked before I stepped out."

"It came out of nowhere," one of the women in the crowd answered. "Ran the red light and sideswiped you. Looked like they didn't even try to hit the brakes. Do you need an ambulance?"

She shook her head. The pain was subsiding to a dull throb, and all she wanted was to get back to the hotel. It was a stupid accident, and she'd probably feel worse tomorrow, but right now adrenaline was shooting through her in the aftermath of the accident.

"Are you sure you don't want somebody to look at you? That was quite a hit you took." Owen loosened the arm he'd wrapped around her waist, not quite letting go, and she steadied herself on her feet.

"I'm fine, really. Can we just go back to the hotel? A

good night's sleep and I'll be ready to rock and roll tomorrow."

"If you're sure." Owen held out his arm. "Why don't you hang onto me until we get there? Just in case." He shot her a rueful smile. "Let me at least make sure nothing else happens on the way back."

The rest of the trip back to the Bellagio was uneventful, if a bit uncomfortable, but she wasn't about to admit that to Owen. He'd been courteous and mindful of her injury, deliberately walking slower so she didn't aggravate her hip and leg. Walking through the lobby, she stopped in front of the elevator. "Thank you for spending the evening with me. You kept me from gorging on junk food and going to bed early and watching way too much TV. I had a nice night."

At least until I got sideswiped by some jerk who needs to take driving lessons.

"My pleasure. You changed my luck, pretty girl. I think maybe I'll head back to the casino before calling it a night. Thank you, it's been…insightful getting to know you."

"Good night, Owen."

The elevator doors opened, and she stepped inside and pressed the button for her floor. As the doors started closing, she heard Owen chuckle.

"Good night, Destiny. Tell Dane I said hello."

An overwhelming sense of dread flooded her, and her blood ran cold when she realized she'd been played for a fool. Stupid her, thinking she'd been playing Owen MacKenna, when all along he'd know who she was, and strung her along like an expert fisherman playing with his catch.

As the elevator rose, her one and only thought played over and over in her head.

Dane's gonna kill me.

CHAPTER TWELVE

DANE PACED ACROSS the living room of the suite for the thousandth time. Where was Destiny? He'd been going out of his mind, wondering if she was okay, then worried she'd gotten herself in way over her head. Owen MacKenna was an unknown commodity. The Owen he remembered from when he was a kid might not be the same person. Life and circumstances changed people. If Owen knew what his father had done, killing two innocent people in cold blood, then he couldn't be trusted. Nothing he'd discovered online indicated Owen was anything more than a devoted son and an astute businessman, overseeing more and more of MacKenna-Duncan's International concerns.

He spun when he heard the door to the suite open, and stood with his arms crossed over his chest, glaring at Destiny. How could she look so sweet and innocent when she defied him and went out with Owen MacKenna?

"Where have you been?" He broke off abruptly when he noticed her limping slightly. "What happened?"

"A run-in with a lousy driver who doesn't know what a red light means. Nothing to worry about. A long, hot soak, and I'll be good to go."

"Where was MacKenna when you were hurt? I'll kill him."

Without waiting for an answer, Dane started for the door, intent on hunting down Owen and tearing him limb from limb. Destiny's soft moan stopped him, forcing him to turn away from the door and rush back to her side.

"Listen, cowboy, Owen never laid a hand on me. Well, he helped me get back here after the car hit me."

"Wait a second? You were hit by a car? What were you doing outside the hotel? I thought you were going to dinner here in the hotel." He scowled, helping her over to the couch and easing her gently onto it. At her wince, he walked to the suite's bar, grabbed a towel and dumped some ice into it, and brought it back, handing it to her. Shooting him a grateful look, she held it to her hip area.

"I was trying to do my job. After dinner, we walked down to The Mirage and watched the volcano show. I asked a few non-intrusive questions, trying to get him to admit anything about his dad that might be suspicious, but he's a closed book. On the way back," she shifted on the couch, wincing and adjusting the ice pack, "we stopped at the corner, waiting for the light to change. When it did, I took a couple of steps, and got clipped by a red-light runner."

Dane eased carefully onto the sofa beside her, making sure not to jostle her. She was making light of her injuries, but he had the feeling she didn't want to share how much she hurt. The thought that the hit-and-run might not have been an accident popped into his head, and he said it aloud before he could stop himself.

She shook her head. "I doubt it. Nobody knew we'd leave the hotel, or where we'd go. It would be hard to orchestrate a drive-by, deliberate hit and run. They'd have a better chance of killing me than injuring me."

"Open your eyes, Destiny. Anybody desperate enough to take out a contract on somebody's life wouldn't hesitate to arrange an accident. All it would have taken was a single phone call or text."

"Dane, I'm too tired to talk about this tonight. Can we do it in the morning? Right now, all I want is to soak in the hottest water I can find, and down a couple of painkillers."

"Of course. I'm sorry. You stay here and rest, I'll go start the bath."

He turned on the water, letting it run hot before engaging the stopper, and filling the tub. He added some scented oil provided by the hotel and went in search of some aspirin or NSAIDs. Filling a glass from the tap, he took the pills out to Destiny and found her asleep on the sofa, her head lolling back against the cushions.

Tonight sealed things for him. He wondered if his quest for justice for his parents outweighed putting somebody he cared about at risk. He didn't believe, not for a second, tonight's hit and run was an accident. Not after somebody had taken a potshot at him a few weeks ago. He was getting close. Close enough that somebody was panicking, and panic made people sloppy.

Putting the glass and pain pills on the coffee table, he slid his arms under Destiny, and lifted her carefully, not wanting her to feel any further pain at his hands. She stirred and opened her eyes, a sleepy smile tugging at her lips.

"You don't have to carry me. I can walk."

"I know you can, but I like having you in my arms, sweetheart. Let me play your Prince Charming tonight and take care of you. Your bath's ready. I found some ibuprofen; maybe it'll take the edge off."

"You're my hero."

"I'm nobody's hero, princess."

Standing beside the bathtub, he reached in and tested the water, making sure it wasn't too hot.

"I'll be right back with that ibuprofen." He needed to get out of there before he gave in to every instinct screaming for him to take her back into his arms and kiss her. Pull her close and make love to her all night long. But that was impossible. Theirs was a business arrangement, a marriage of convenience, a means to an end. He couldn't change the rules in the middle of the game. It wouldn't be fair. She was hurt and vulnerable, and he wasn't a jerk who'd take advantage of a woman when her defenses were down.

When he came back, she was standing exactly where he left her, looking soft and vulnerable, and he'd never wanted her more.

"Here." He handed her the ibuprofen and the water glass.

"I'll be right outside if you need anything."

She shot him a grateful look and handed him the glass. "Thank you, Dane."

"I was going to tell you earlier, but plans changed. Since my brothers showed up, I need to get back to Shiloh Springs and let Momma and Dad know what's going on. Tell them the whole truth. You get some rest. We're heading for the airport after breakfast."

She blinked her beautiful blue eyes, and he read first confusion, followed by resignation. Did she regret leaving? Marrying him?

"I'll be ready."

"Good. Holler if you need anything."

"I'm fine, really. Go to bed. I'll see you in the morning."

He walked out of the bathroom, pulling the door closed behind him. Didn't matter what she said, he wasn't going to bed until he knew she was tucked up into hers, safe and sound. Even then, he doubted he'd sleep. Between wanting her, needing her, and thinking about the accident that might have taken her away from him permanently.

It was going to be a long night.

CHAPTER THIRTEEN

D ANE PULLED HIS pickup in front of his parents' home and cut the engine. Destiny had been uncharacteristically silent on the drive from the airport. They'd decided the night before to tell his folks everything when they got home. Now that Shiloh, Heath, and Antonio knew all the facts, it was past time for his parents to know about his past. And his goal to take down Matthew MacKenna.

"You ready?"

She gave a brief nod. "Why does it feel like I'm about to face a firing squad?"

"Don't worry, Momma and Dad won't be mad at you. Pretty sure their ire is going to be solely directed at me."

"Is that supposed to make me feel better? I respect your parents, and I've done nothing but go behind their backs from the moment I started checking out the Boudreaus. I mean, I only did it to make sure nobody did anything to hurt your family, but things snowballed into—"

"Take a breath, princess. They will understand why you did what you did. Working with Shiloh, you became friends. You care about him and by extension, them. Chances are they'll be grateful you're using your skills, your abilities, to undermine any possible threat to them or their children. Momma, especially, will approve." Under his breath, he muttered the word, "eventually."

The front door of the Big House opened, and his dad stepped onto the porch, his steely gaze focused on Dane's truck like a laser. Uh-oh, Dad wasn't happy. Guess his brothers beat them home. They'd snuck out of the hotel several hours before Dane and Destiny, leaving a message they were heading home. He just bet Antonio couldn't wait to spill everything to his folks the second he'd gotten back.

"Time to face the music." Dane nodded toward the house, and Destiny's eyes widened when she spotted his father standing just outside the front door, arms crossed over his chest. He had to admit, his father was an intimidating sight.

"I think I'd rather be covered with honey and tied to a fire ant hill."

Climbing from the truck, Dane walked around the front and frowned when Destiny climbed down before he could open her door. He took her hand, threading his fingers through hers. Might as well present a united front from the start, before they faced the third degree sure to come.

Stepping up onto the porch, he said, "Good morning, Dad."

"Son. Hello, Destiny."

"Mr. Boudreau." At his sudden frown, she quickly said,

"I mean Douglas."

"That's better. Dane, your mother's waiting for y'all in the kitchen." Spinning on his heel, he walked into the house and straight for the kitchen, Dane and Destiny following. Several voices, both male and female, came from the living room, ceasing instantly when Dane walked into the entryway.

"Momma." Dane pulled his mother into a hug, felt her stiff body against his before she relaxed, and wrapped her arms around him. With that simple action, he knew everything was going to be okay. She might be mad with him, but she never held onto her anger long. She was too loving and forgiving. The rest of the world might see her as a strong, competent businessperson—which she totally was—but inside she was a big softie who loved her family and her friends with a fierceness and protectiveness of a mother bear with her cubs.

"Don't you 'Momma' me, Dane. I'm furious with you. How could you keep something like this from us?"

Going right for the jugular.

"It's a long story."

The disapproving look she shot him, along with the hands on her hips, told Dane more than words she wasn't going to be placated with some simplistic excuse. She demanded and deserved better.

"Momma—"

"How hard was it to tell me you were getting married?

Really? You run off to Las Vegas without a word? I expected better from you, Dane Boudreau. You've always been my responsible son. The dependable one who could be counted on to do what was right. And, poof, you up and run off with Destiny."

Wait, didn't she know about MacKenna? He'd figured his brothers would have blabbed the minute they got home. Not so much to get him in trouble, but simply to give them sufficient time to acclimate to the information that Dane remembered his past and hadn't told them. Instead, she was upset about him getting married and not telling her?

"And you." Momma turned her disapproving stare at Destiny. "How did this one convince you to run away with him?"

"Um...he asked me?" Destiny shot him a *you better handle this* glare, and he felt the corner of his lips curl.

"How about everybody sit down, and I'll pour us some coffee and explain everything?" Dane led his mother to the kitchen table and pulled out a chair. He did the same for Destiny and then turned to the cupboard, pulling down several mugs. Checking the coffee pot, it was full, which he'd known it would be. It was rare to find an empty pot in this house. The only time that happened was when nobody was home; otherwise, there always an endless supply of caffeine available.

After passing around the mugs, he sat facing his father. "How much did Antonio tell you?"

"Nothing. He said you'd explain everything when you got here. He did ask us to be patient and listen. Guess you've got quite a story to tell us."

He wasn't sure if he should thank his brother or curse him. It would have been easier facing his parents this morning, with them already knowing everything. But he'd been the one to keep the secret, first as a scared kid who didn't trust anybody, and later because he wanted to have all the answers first.

"Story later. I want to know when the two of you fell in love and decided eloping was better than having a wedding here in Shiloh Springs with your family present."

Oh, yeah, Momma ain't happy.

"Mrs. Boudreau, I promise it wasn't like that. None of this was meant to hurt either of you or his family. Things moved really fast, and we needed to…"

"Make things official," Dane added. "There are things I need to tell you. Please, Momma, Dad, I need you to understand that nothing I've done was meant to hurt either of you. I did it to protect you and my family."

His dad sat up a little straighter in his chair, though he didn't say anything. Dane knew he had his father's full attention. Fortunately, his father was the type of man who listened and got all the facts before he acted.

"I promised your brothers we'd listen before we made any judgments." His momma patted his hand. It was such a motherly thing, his voice locked in his throat and he swallowed hard. "Not about the marriage, because I've got plenty to say about that. But Antonio said you had good reasons for your actions, so I'm going to withhold judgment until you've explained."

"Thank you, Momma."

"I reserve the right to give you a piece of my mind if I think you've done something astronomically stupid though."

Destiny snorted back a laugh at his mother's words.

"Explain, son. We'll listen with an open mind."

"I'm not sure where to start. Everything goes back to when I first came to live with you." Dane wasn't surprised when he saw his father clasp his mother's hand and squeeze it gently. The love between his parents was a rare and special thing. In a world where affection and marriage, a commitment of any kind, was disposable and people moved on to their next relationship, his parents were an example that true love, true companionship, was not only achievable but something to be desired and sought. Maybe someday he'd share that with someone special. He couldn't help glancing toward Destiny, not surprised she'd spotted his father's gentle movement too.

"I never told you, never told anybody, but when I came to live here I remembered who I was."

"What? Dane—"

"Sweetheart, we promised to listen without interrupting. Let him explain." His mother's lips compressed into an unhappy line, and guilt swamped him. Even though he'd known it was going to be hard, it felt like a thousand pounds sat in the center of his chest, and he could barely breathe. The hurt reflected in his mother's eyes was almost his undoing. It wrecked him, and he couldn't help wondering if she'd ever be able to forgive him.

"Let me go back. There was a wonderful woman named Ginger. She was my babysitter. My tutor. She was young and fun and so full of life. She'd been going to college, getting her degree in education, and took care of me to not only make some extra money but also for free room and board. My parents…"

Dane swallowed when he said the words because Douglas and Patricia Boudreau were his parents. The parents he loved more than anything else in the world. They'd raised him, taught him, disciplined him when needed, and loved him with their whole hearts. Peter and Marjorie Duncan had loved him too, but their memory was clouded with the passage of years and a child's affection toward their mom and dad.

"His biological parents. They are a big part of his story, but never believe for an instant that you and Douglas aren't Dane's parents in every sense of the word." Destiny's soft-spoken defense of him, as well as assurance to his parents, sent a tingling warmth flooding through him. Even after everything she'd been through the last few days, she still put him first.

"Ginger became my lifeline, my only friend. When my

biological parents were killed—"

"No!" His mother's whispered exclamation almost broke him again. But he couldn't stop. If he did, he might not ever be able to tell them everything.

"They'd been out to a business party, something they did from time to time. Ginger stayed home with me. We heard them come into the house when they got home, but they didn't call out or come upstairs—which they always did. Ginger must have heard something because she told me to be quiet and looked over the railing at the top of the stairs. All I remember is her grabbing me and running for the back door, telling me I had to be quiet as a mouse. I thought we were playing a game, like hide and seek."

His father's arm went around his mom's shoulder, lending his nonverbal support. Dane knew he needed to keep this brief, get the story told. He could give them all the details later when the shock had a chance to wear off.

"She drove all night, only stopping long enough to get gas and for bathroom breaks at rest areas. I doubt she slept for the first forty-eight hours after we ran. She finally told me my parents were dead. The one thing she said over and over, like a mantra she'd memorized, was it wasn't my fault. Looking back now, it's obvious she saw their deaths, witnessed whoever killed them. She never told me who did it. Every night before we went to bed, she'd remind me how much they loved me, how important I was, and that she'd always protect me."

"Sounds like she was quite a woman, son. Why didn't she go to the police, tell them what she saw?" Douglas' question was softly voiced, and Dane knew his father was trying to hold onto his temper. Nothing enraged Douglas Boudreau faster than injustice and somebody hurting a child. His father's unwavering honesty had rubbed off on all his children, which explained why most of them were in some form of law enforcement or positioned in places where helping others overcome problems was their priority.

"She was, Dad. She didn't have to take on the responsibility of trying to protect a six-year-old, alone in the world, and possibly in the crosshairs of a killer herself. Yet she never once made me feel like I was a burden or an unwanted responsibility."

Dane grabbed hold of Destiny's hand, feeling the need for an anchor, drowning in memories of the past, and she was there, a touchstone to keep him centered. Telling somebody about Ginger felt like an ache in his heart. The only other person he'd talked to about the kindhearted woman was Destiny. He'd left that part of the story out when he'd talked with his brothers in Las Vegas. But his parents deserved to know there were other people out there, like them, who put aside their own lives to help a scared little boy who'd lost everything.

"We moved around all the time, not staying in any place longer than a few weeks at most. Ginger would get a part-time job, usually working fast food or waitressing someplace.

Sometimes she cleaned rooms at the hotels where we stayed, to keep a roof over our heads and food on the table. She always made it into a game, tried to keep it fun. I wasn't unhappy to be with Ginger, but I didn't know any better. Except I missed my parents and wanted to go home. I couldn't go to school, because we never landed anyplace long enough, and she was terrified about not leaving a paper trail. We changed our names. I was Johnny when we were in Aspen. Jacob when we made it to Santa Fe. By the time we landed in Amarillo, I was Daniel."

He didn't dare look at his mother, because he knew he'd lose it if he did. The indrawn gasp when he'd mentioned Ginger, the way his father scooted his chair closer? There'd be tears in her eyes for a woman she'd never met. His mother had a heart as big as Texas, filled with compassion for everyone. Didn't matter if she'd known you all her life or were a complete stranger, she was always there to lend a helping hand with an open heart.

"The owner of the motel where we stayed called the police when Ginger hadn't come home after two days. I didn't know until later they'd found Ginger's body in an alley by a dumpster. The cops called it a drug deal gone bad. Nobody listened when a little boy told them his friend didn't take nasty drugs. That's what Ginger called 'em. As far as the police knew, she was simply another unidentified body to turn over to the coroner's office. When they wanted to know where my parents were, I didn't tell them anything. I couldn't. I'd made Ginger a promise never to tell anybody what happened. So, I stopped talking."

"I remember," his mother whispered. "CPS and the doctors said there wasn't anything physically wrong with you, that it had to be shock and fear. It took forever for you to talk. But this? Baby, you remembered all this and never said anything. We thought you couldn't remember anything before you came to live with us. The counselor with CPS said it was possible you'd never remember who you were or where you came from. It was all a lie?"

Dane took a deep breath before answering. "Not an intentional lie. After Ginger died, and I ended up in foster care, everything got muddled up in my head. All the unfamiliar faces, new people, I buried everything deep, so I didn't have to think about it. I never told anybody. When I realized I was in a safe place, for the first time in a long time, I wanted to forget. You and Dad, you made me feel special again, the way my biological parents had. I didn't want to lose that feeling, and I knew if I said anything, the bad people might come and take me back. To a six-year-old kid who finally found a home, it's the stuff of nightmares."

"You could have told us."

Dane turned to face Rafe, who stood in the kitchen doorway, Tessa by his side. Lucas stood one step behind him, with his arm around Jill's waist. He wondered how much they'd heard. Knowing his brothers, they'd probably stood there the whole time, listening. Not condemning. Every

Boudreau son had their own grief, their own childhood trauma, and they understood and accepted he was no different. Destiny's hand squeezed his, and he realized he really was home.

"I know. There's a lot more, and I'll tell you later. But for the last ten years, maybe more, I've been searching, digging everywhere, trying to figure out who had a motive to kill my biological parents. I've looked at every article written about them. Done internet searches. I even hired a private investigator to see what they could dig up."

Rafe snorted. "Please let me be there when you tell Shiloh you hired an outsider when your brother is one of the best in the business." Rafe's laugh broke the tension which hung in the air.

"He was busy chasing down leads on Renee. I think I can be forgiven since he ended up with the woman he loves. Besides, he already knows. I told him when he showed up in Vegas."

"Tell them the rest or I will." Destiny's voice reminded him he hadn't finished telling his parents everything.

"I think the PI must have stumbled upon something that alerted somebody who'd set up an internet flag, because it wasn't long after that I found out somebody was looking for me. The real me, not Dane Boudreau."

"That's right, we don't even know your real name."

"It's Thomas. Thomas Elliot Duncan."

Rafe cursed. "The missing kid from Denver? Heir to the

Duncan fortune and half of MacKenna-Duncan International? That Thomas Elliot Duncan?"

"Yeah."

"Dane, stop stalling," Destiny chided.

"Remember the party, celebrating Derrick and Daisy's engagement? Destiny called me that night with some info she'd found on the web." He nodded to Destiny, indicating she should tell them what she found.

"Ever since I started working with Shiloh, and met all of you, I kind of keep watch on the internet for any mention of your names. Sort of a just in case anything happens precaution. One of my alerts triggered on Dane's name that night, from a site on the dark web. A professional mercenary site. Somebody was offering a lot of money to kill Dane."

There were gasps from Tessa and Jill, with vehement curses from Rafe and Douglas. Dane hadn't wanted them to know, but if, as he suspected, things were escalating, they might all be in danger simply as collateral damage. He wouldn't leave them unprepared.

"Who?" This from Douglas.

"I don't know. I'm still digging deeper, but it's buried under a ton of data, with everything so far coming up anonymous. But," Destiny's stark tone almost made Dane cringe, "Trust me, I'm not going to stop until I know who is willing to pay almost a quarter of a million dollars to kill my husband."

CHAPTER FOURTEEN

DESTINY WALKED BESIDE Dane around the side of the Big House. They'd had a day back to settle in after dropping their bombshell news on his family, as well as telling Douglas and Ms. Patti about somebody trying to kill their son. She was surprised Dane wasn't currently wrapped from head to toe in bubble wrap and tucked away someplace safe. She wouldn't put it past Ms. Patti to haul him off if she got even a whiff of somebody getting too close for comfort to her baby boy.

Add in the fact she and Dane got married, eloped without telling her and she'd just found out about it, Destiny felt lucky Ms. Patti had welcomed her into the family. Of course, Dane hadn't explained the real reason he'd married her. As far as the Boudreaus were concerned, she and Dane were deeply in love and planning to spend the rest of their lives together.

Stop tormenting yourself wishing for something that'll never happen. Be happy with today and figure out how you're going to have a life once your investigation is over.

After lunch, Dane mentioned he wanted to show her

something special. Intrigued, she couldn't help being curious about whatever it was he wanted to show her. He'd given her this mysterious smile, like he harbored a secret he wanted to share. Oh, well, what was one more secret between them?

"Where are we going?"

"It's not far. I promise you're going to love it."

They curved around the patio built onto the side of the Big House, where there was a seating area set up, with a bistro table and chairs, and an abundance of colorful pots overflowing with flowers and greenery. She wondered if this was Ms. Patti's doing. Tina had mentioned Ms. Patti had a green thumb and loved to garden. How she managed to, with her jam-packed schedule, was mind-blowing. Every time she spent more than five minutes with Dane's mother, she realized the woman was a ball of energy, always moving, always one step ahead.

Cutting across a grassy patch, Dane pointed toward a stand of tall pines. "It's just through there."

Walking several feet into the trees, she stepped through a natural opening—into wonderland. It looked like a scene from a fairytale. A painted white gazebo occupied the center of a cleared area, its rounded rooftop reaching toward the sky. Roses and ivy climbed up the sides, and she inhaled deeply, smiling at the wonderful floral and woodsy scent. The occasional pine needles on the dirt floor added to the natural beauty.

"This is amazing. I could sit here for hours. There's such

a sense of peace." She turned to face him. "It's your mother's, right?"

"Good guess. Dad built the gazebo for her years ago. Wanted her to have her own special place, away from all the craziness of raising eleven kids. And, you have to admit, with our family there's always some kind of drama going on."

"You mean like one of her sons eloping to Vegas without telling her?"

She watched him, looking for any sign of regret, but the only thing she spotted was his answering grin.

"I plead the fifth."

She took a few steps closer to the gazebo and made a move to walk inside. Dane reached past her shoulder and flipped a switch, and the interior exploded with light. Tiny fairy lights, the kind she thought of as Christmas tree lights, ringed around the inside of the roof, illuminating the well in the center of the structure. Made of rocks and wood, it reminded her of a wishing well she'd seen as a kid, the kind with a rope and bucket that lowered down to the water.

"Do I get to make a wish?"

Instead of answering, he pulled a quarter from his pocket and handed it to her. "Hope it comes true."

Closing her eyes, she wished for the one thing she knew she couldn't have. Her impossible dream.

"Me, too," she whispered.

She ran her hand along the top of the well, walking around it, before moving to sit on one of the benches that rested against the interior walls. She hadn't lied; this place really was peaceful.

"Dad and some of us helped run electricity out here, so Momma could stay here as long as she wanted, day or night. This place is special to her. The roses and other flowers you saw around the base—she and Rafe spent days planting them."

"Rafe?"

"Yeah, he likes to garden. Something he has in common with Momma. I definitely don't have a green thumb. Put me around cattle and horses, and I can deal with anything. I even breathe on a potted plant, and it dies."

"Something we have in common. I've had friends give me plants they swear can't be killed. I always prove them wrong. If I want flowers in my apartment, I buy them at the florist. Who am I kidding, I pick them up at the grocery store along with my TV dinners."

"You know, this place has a bit of history besides being Momma's secret oasis." He moved from the doorway and sat beside her. "If we find somebody special, somebody we want to share our background, or childhood with, we bring them to the gazebo."

A strange, tingling warmth filled her. Did that mean he considered her somebody special? Yes, they were married, but it was a business affair, a way to ensure MacKenna paid for his transgressions and didn't consider killing Dane. She was still a little fuzzy on why Dane thought marriage was necessary, but he'd wanted it. So had she, but for different reasons. Reasons she'd never admit to her sexy cowboy.

"You already know everything there is to know about me, princess, but I know almost nothing about you. I'd like to, if you're willing to share."

The warm feeling she'd experienced only moments before disappeared, and a chill stole over her. She wasn't ready, might never be ready, because the truth wasn't pretty. She couldn't dress it up with a bow and shout *this is me, no flaws, no issues.*

She'd dreaded this moment, even as she'd known it was coming. Not even Shiloh knew the whole truth, and he knew more about her than anybody in Shiloh Springs.

Dane must have sensed something from her unnerving silence because he reached up to cup her cheek. "If it upsets you too much, you don't have to tell me."

"It's okay. It's not a happy story. Most people have rough patches in their lives, right? Your family is the perfect example of overcoming the odds life throws at you and coming out the other side better."

"We're the lucky ones," Dane agreed. "I thank God every day I ended up with Momma and Dad. I'd even go so far as to include my whole passel of brothers and Nica, but don't tell them I said that. My situation could have ended up so much worse. Being adopted by the Boudreaus, belonging to a real, loving family? I hope someday I can help others, the way they helped me and my brothers."

She could picture it. Dane seated atop a horse with a couple of boys on ponies at his side, riding the ranch and teaching his sons to be fine young men. Exactly the way Douglas and Ms. Patti did with him and all their boys. Dane wouldn't care if they were his biological kids; he'd love them anyway. Knew it deep in her gut, and she admired him all the more for it.

"Princess?"

"She gave a rueful smile. "Sorry, I was a million miles away."

"Wherever it was, it must've made you happy. You were smiling."

"Okay, let's talk. Before we start, I'm just gonna say this once. Don't feel sorry for me. My life wasn't pretty before I came to Shiloh Springs, but it made me the person I am. Good and bad, warts and all."

He studied her face and slowly nodded. "I promise."

Blowing out a deep breath, Destiny stood, taking a couple of steps toward the well. She couldn't tell him everything, bare her soul, being so close, within touching distance of the man she was falling for.

Who am I kidding? I'm totally head over heels, never coming back from it, in love with Dane Boudreau. And it scares me half to death.

"I lived a not so pristine life when I was younger. As a teenager, I liked to party. The friends I hung out with were the party crowd. When I was seventeen, every weekend was a long binge of drinking and dancing. We hung out with the football team because they always had booze. I smoked a little weed sometimes, but didn't really care for it. It didn't give me the same buzz I got from alcohol. When I drank, I got reckless. Bold in a way I wasn't when I was sober."

She perched on the edge of the well, kicking her feet back and forth, her heels brushing lightly against the rocks. She couldn't look at Dane, because she didn't want to see the disgust on his face.

"My girlfriends didn't mind doing the hard stuff. Coke, meth, it was readily available, and nobody gave a second thought to its legality. I'm telling you so you'll understand my mindset back then. I was all about having a good time. My home life wasn't horrible. I had friends who were in abusive situations, but I lived with my mom, and she never raised a hand to me. She wasn't home long enough, because she was working two, and sometimes three jobs. Like I said, no different than most kids."

She paused and for the first time looked up, her gaze caught in his. His face was expressionless, a blank mask she couldn't read.

"My best friend and I were so alike it was scary. We liked the same things: computers, boys, and booze. Heck, we lived for Friday nights, because that meant endless partying. Mary's boyfriend was a senior, on the football team. Huge and not the nicest guy, but she loved him. I thought he was a jerk but tolerated him because of Mary."

Goosebumps crawled across her skin when she pictured Vic. Six foot three, two hundred and thirty pounds, he'd towered over Mary, and he'd loved to point out their size difference, claiming he could break her as easily as a twig. Destiny hated Vic, not only for breaking her friend's heart but for what he'd done to Mary.

"Vic was a controlling jackass. He didn't want Mary to do anything without his permission. I think he'd have told her when to breathe if he could've. I can't count the number of times I found her covering bruises with long sleeves or sweaters. She never blamed him. Always made excuses. He was stressed because they lost the game. His parents took away his car. There was always something that set his temper on edge, and he took it out on her. It took me a long time to put two and two together, because Mary never said a word, never blamed Vic. And I was oblivious because I drank so much, I didn't realize my best friend was being knocked around."

"Destiny, you were a kid."

"I was old enough to drink myself into oblivion. I was old enough to get behind the wheel of a car after drinking so much I could barely see the lines in the road. I was old enough to mow down my best friend's boyfriend with my car and kill him."

Dane's lack of reaction at her statement surprised her. Hadn't he heard her? Understood that she'd killed a man? While she hadn't planned it, the result was the loss of life and the destruction of her soul.

"Destiny—"

"Don't. If you say anything, I won't be able to finish, and you need to know everything. That night, the team lost the homecoming game, so everybody felt lousy. The party at the quarry—that's where we'd go on Friday nights—was subdued. Mary and I went with a couple friends. Mary made a beeline for Vic, who'd already started drinking before we got there. I didn't know he'd also snorted cocaine after the game, which made him volatile. He and Mary disappeared, and I didn't think anything about it. They usually ended up in the backseat of Vic's car and had sex. I grabbed a beer and danced around the fire somebody had started. One beer led to two, then three. I'm not sure how much time passed when I spotted Mary stumbling toward me. She was crying, a total mess. Her nose was bloody and one eye was swollen shut. Bruises around her throat. I lost it, went completely off the rails. I'm not sure what I was going to do, except hunt down Vic. Guy outweighed me by over a hundred pounds, but I wasn't thinking straight. Nothing mattered except finding Vic and giving him a taste of his own medicine. Fueled by fury and alcohol, I started toward Vic's car, only Mary stopped me. She grabbed my arm and pleaded with me to get her out of there. Begged me to take her home."

Hopping down off the well, she began to walk around it, her hand skimming across the surface. The rocks used to build the well were smooth with age, almost polished to a shine. Their coolness beneath her fingers helped her focus, keep talking, instead of racing back to the Big House to hide. She hated that she'd been weak and foolish. Being young wasn't an excuse. What happened that night changed her, honed her into a sharp blade, one who worked hard every day to atone for her past by making sure her future counted for something.

"Mary was a mess. My only thought was to get her to the emergency room. She refused to go because she didn't want Vic to get in trouble. Even though he'd choked her, broken her nose, and blackened her eye, she still defended him. Tried to make excuses for what he'd done. Like there's ever an excuse for a man using his fists against a woman. We argued. I know I shouldn't have gotten behind the wheel, but I wasn't thinking straight. Mary begged me to take her to my house first, help her get cleaned up before she went home. I caved and pulled out of the parking lot. I never saw Vic step in front of the car, not until it was too late. Honestly, I don't remember the details. It all happened so fast; it was a blur. Depending on who you talked to, some of the people who witnessed the accident said I swerved into Vic deliberately. Others said Mary grabbed the steering wheel and pointed us at Vic. I remember the thud of Vic's body hitting the car, seeing him roll across the hood and fall to the ground."

"He died." Dane's quietly spoken words helped Destiny know he understood what she was telling him, and why she wasn't going to go into all the bloody details.

She nodded at his words. "The paramedics said he died instantly. Mary and I both were taken to the police station. I answered questions for what felt like hours. They did a blood alcohol test, and I was over the legal limit. Mary's test was clean because she hadn't started drinking. She went off with Vic for their rendezvous. Besides, she hadn't been the one behind the wheel. Considering how she looked, the cops knew something happened. The worst part, though, was Mary told the cops I deliberately steered into Vic. That I intended to hit him."

"In other words, she lied."

"Yeah. Not only was I terrified I'd go to prison, but I'd also lost my best friend. They arrested me, booked me, and put me in a cell."

The memory of that night still haunted her, gave her nightmares where she'd wake up sweating in a panic. Her counselor had called it PTSD. Destiny called it reality. Alone and scared, she'd huddled on the corner of the stainless-steel cot attached to the wall, rocking back and forth, her knees tucked under her chin. Nobody would tell her what was happening or even what charges she faced. She'd been naïve, young, and had never been in serious trouble before. The closest she'd come was shoplifting makeup, which hadn't seemed like a big deal at the time. She'd cried, hoping it was all a mistake. The accident had been precisely that—an accident. Only the authorities and Vic's family didn't agree.

"You must have been terrified." Dane hadn't moved from his seat, though she noted the whiteness of his knuckles gripping the bench. "I can't imagine what it must've been like."

"It was awful. I answered all their questions because I didn't know I should have had a lawyer present. And, yes, they read me my Miranda rights. I was in shock, still a little drunk, and the reality of what happened hadn't sunk in. I ended up with a public defender. I lucked out and got somebody who actually cared about what happened to me. She was amazing. I'd be in prison right now if she hadn't gone to bat for me. The first thing she nailed them with was questioning a minor without a parent or legal guardian being present. The second was questioning me without the benefit of counsel. The police tried to claim I never asked for a lawyer, but that didn't hold up, because again I was a minor. My mom," Destiny drew in a ragged breath before continuing. "My arrest hit her hard. She'd done everything for me, being a single parent, and making sure I had everything I needed, and now I was putting her through a different kind of nightmare. One she'd never imagined possible."

"We don't have control of every aspect of our lives, sweetheart. Things happen around us all the time that we can't control."

"I know, but this was a blow she hadn't expected. It broke her spirit. She was there, supporting me through the depositions and hearings, but she wasn't there, if you know what I mean. If it hadn't been for Lois, my public defender, I'd probably be behind bars today. I ended up with negligent involuntary manslaughter charges and could have faced prison time. Luckily, Lois convinced Mary to tell the truth about grabbing the wheel, which contributed to the accident."

Destiny looked past Dane, surprised to see the beginning of dusk falling. They'd been there longer than she'd thought. Yet the heavy weight she'd carried, holding this time in her life close, wrapped around her heart, seemed to have eased. Time to finish it, and hope Dane didn't think less of her.

"Lois convinced the district attorney to make a deal. One year probation and a seventy-five hundred dollar fine. Once the time was served, my record would be expunged, and it would be like it never happened. Lois cited extenuating circumstances for the accident, and between Mary telling the truth and the photographs the police took of Mary's injuries the night everything happened—well, I got lucky."

"And now you're here." Dane stood and moved to stand in front of her, his hands cupping her cheeks. He gently brushed away the teardrops she hadn't realized she'd shed.

"Yeah. I tried staying in California, but everything was a reminder of what happened. Once I'd served my probation, I graduated from high school and got a job. I swore I'd pay my mom back every penny of the seventy-five hundred dollars. She wasn't the same after what happened. Something inside her shut down. I think seeing me every day was a reminder of what she called her failure. No matter what I said or did, I couldn't break through to her. I think part of her gave up, and it was my fault. I was a walking, talking reminder of my mistakes, so I left. Traveled up and down the state, taking jobs wherever I landed. I finally landed an entry-level computer job, basic stuff, simple data entry. I loved working on the computer. I felt at home with my hands on a keyboard. One of the guys working in the IT department took me under his wing and started teaching me. I learned how to write code, how to debug, and when the time was right, he showed me how to get into places through back doors. To hack sites. Mostly for fun, but once I got a taste for it, I was hooked."

"My little hacker." The words were said with a touch of humor, the smile tugging his lips lifting her spirits. If he could joke after everything she'd told him, maybe she hadn't ruined everything. Dane had a loving, forgiving soul, and she hoped it would extend to her because it would destroy her if he walked away.

"I got really good at everything related to digging up information. It's like solving a puzzle, finding all the pieces, and making them fit. Once I started seriously working with computers, there was no turning back. I took courses and worked with others to learn everything I could about cybersecurity and discovered all the secrets the World Wide Web held. Which is how I met your brother, and he offered me a job."

"I'm glad he did. Otherwise, I'd never have met you." He tugged on a lock of her hair, before adding, "That would have been a shame, Mrs. Boudreau."

"Would it?"

"Thank you for sharing your life with me, princess. I treasure your honesty, and I'll keep your secrets."

"Thank you."

"I think I mentioned it's kind of a tradition for the Boudreaus to bring somebody special to the gazebo, to share its magic. But I didn't tell you there's also another tradition we Boudreaus have about this gazebo. Something else we like to share."

"Really?"

"Uh-huh." There was a distinctive twinkle in his eyes, one that made Destiny a tiny bit leery.

"What's that?"

"This."

He pulled her into his arms and kissed her.

CHAPTER FIFTEEN

D ANE OPENED THE front door to find Antonio, Heath, Shiloh, and Liam standing on the porch. Other than Liam, the others had stayed behind in Vegas, keeping an eye on Matthew and Owen MacKenna, and studying the pile of evidence he'd left with them. Antonio shoved past him and the others followed.

"Coffee. Tell me there's coffee."

"Heath, you've had three cups already. You're gonna be climbing the walls if you don't slow down." "Antonio shot his brother a glare at his answering growl and threw up his hands. "Fine, but don't blame me when Camilla switches you to decaf."

"Ha. She already tried that. Trust me, she switched back to the regular stuff pretty darned quick. Too many years of living on caffeine makes me grouchy when I don't get my fix."

"Guys, keep it down. Destiny's sleeping."

Three sets of eyes turned in his direction. "She's living here?" Antonio asked the question first.

"Where else would she be? She's my wife."

"We know that, doofus. But you said in Vegas this marriage was a business deal, not a romantic match."

"How are we supposed to convince MacKenna it's a real marriage if she lives halfway across town? Besides, it's easier to do research if we're in the same place. It only makes sense."

No way was he telling his nosy brothers he liked having Destiny around. She was fun, interesting, and had a wicked sense of humor. When they weren't online digging up any info they could on his parents' deaths and scrutinizing the files on Matthew MacKenna, they'd spent time together. They liked the same movies and TV shows. Although when it came to books, they were a million miles apart. He liked mysteries and sci-fi, military thrills. Destiny didn't mind mysteries, though she preferred cozy mysteries. But he found out she liked romances. Her e-reader was loaded with tons of happily-ever-after books, including owning every one of Camilla's books.

Dane led the way into the kitchen and poured four large mugs and pulled a container of milk from the fridge. Sugar was on the counter, if anybody wanted it, they could get it themselves. He wasn't their maid.

Heath gave a satisfied sigh after taking a huge gulp of his coffee. "Ah, that hits the spot. Anyway, bro, I wanted to let you know I looked at some video footage from a store near where Destiny was hit. Made you a copy. Emailed it to you."

"Find anything?"

Heath nodded. "Looks like the car that hit Destiny deliberately ran the red light. The driver braked, slowed down before deliberately rounding the corner and clipping her with the bumper. It was a low-speed impact; otherwise, she'd have been hurt worse than the bruising she sustained."

"I looked at the footage and agree with Heath. I'm no expert, but the way the driver slowed, it was a calculated action." Liam raised his mug to Dane, before taking a sip.

A throat cleared behind him, and he knew Destiny heard Liam's statement. Had she heard Heath's, too?

"Good morning, sweetheart. The guys showed up looking for coffee."

"Uh-huh. Where's mine?"

Dane immediately handed her his mug, and she smiled her thanks before taking a sip. At Heath's snicker, he realized what he'd done. They'd taken to sharing things, mostly in the evenings. A big bowl of popcorn, his secret stash of peanut M&Ms. It had been a subconscious move on his part, but he knew his brothers would read more into than it meant.

"I heard what you said. My question is why would somebody want to deliberately hurt me?"

"I have a theory on that." Antonio stood and offered Destiny his chair, and she slid onto the seat. Dane felt like an idiot. He should have given her his. Or let her sit on his lap.

"What are you thinking?"

"Well, Sis, I think somebody wanted to distract Dane—

and you—from digging too deep. If he's focused on watching your back, making sure nobody's after you, he's not thinking about finding evidence about his parents' decades-old murder."

Dane started at Antonio's use of the familial endearment. It was one more indication that his brother accepted his relationship with Destiny. Most his brothers were happily ensconced in relationships with amazing women. Some days, he felt a touch of the green-eyed monster raise its ugly head, and he wondered if he'd ever be lucky enough to find his soul mate, his perfect match.

Looking at Destiny, he realized he already had. And she was his wife.

Before he could make a total fool of himself, there was another knock on the door. Since he wasn't expecting anyone, not even the knuckleheads who currently had just invaded his kitchen, he headed for the door, glancing out the window before opening it. After hearing somebody deliberately tried to run down Destiny, he wasn't taking any chances.

A middle-aged man in a courier uniform stood outside the door, a cardboard envelope and an electronic clipboard in his hand.

Opening the door, Dane signed for the package, and carried it into the kitchen, tapping it against his hand.

"What's that?" Liam stood at the counter, refilling his mug with the last of the coffee. Without asking, he started gathering the things he needed to make another pot. See, he always knew Liam was the smart brother. Smart enough to realize they weren't close to being finished with their impromptu meeting and would need caffeinated fuel.

"No idea." He quirked a brow when he noted the return address was completely illegible. Was that deliberate?

Ripping open the zip closure, he pulled out a single sheet of paper. And stared at the message. In large, bold print, all caps, it read:

YOU'RE LOOKING IN THE WRONG PLACE.

Beneath the message was a computer link. A single URL, one he didn't recognize.

Without a word, Destiny rose and left the kitchen, returning moments later with her laptop. Her fingers flew across the keys, and her eyes widened at whatever she saw on the screen.

"Guys, you're not going to believe this!" Excitement laced her words, and she swiveled the laptop around, so he and his brothers could view the screen. His mouth fell open at what he was seeing.

"Are you serious?"

"How did we not know about this?"

"No way!"

All his brothers spoke at the same time, sounding as shocked as he felt. Dane's gaze caught Destiny's, and she gave him a timid yet satisfied smile, like she'd just slid the final piece of a jigsaw puzzle into place and could see the whole picture.

"Bro, you've got to find out where this package came from because I want to shake the hand of the guy who sent this." Liam stood and clapped Dane on the back. "I've got to get to the job site, and I'm already late, but keep me posted on what you find. You need me, text."

"Thanks, Liam."

Antonio grabbed the courier envelope and pulled out his phone. "Y'all keep digging into that website. I'm going to see where this package came from. Might give us a clue who sent it."

Dane ignored his brother, leaning over Destiny's shoulder to stare at the computer screen. The link led to a site he'd never seen before, would never have known it existed without the anonymous sender's help.

Outside of Destiny and his brothers, nobody knew he was digging into MacKenna. But somebody else knew, and they'd decided to help him take down the MacKenna patriarch.

Destiny scrolled through page after page of documents. A few documents outlined egregious actions by Matthew MacKenna. But what surprised him were the files on his son. It looked like Junior cleaned up all his daddy's messes, along with committing a few of his own.

Two files were interrogations by the police after his parents' murders. One for Matthew and one for sixteen-year-old

Owen. Files Dane hadn't been able to access. They hadn't been on the police server. When he'd requested all the information related to the Duncan case, through official and unofficial channels, he'd been turned away empty-handed.

Naturally, Matthew and Owen alibied each other. Sketchy but possible. Matthew could have convinced a gullible sixteen-year-old to lie for him, especially if he meant keeping his father out of prison.

"There's a lot of stuff here, Dane. It's gonna take a while to go through everything, but there's a gold mine of information. More than enough to give you a legitimate shot at taking over MacKenna-Duncan. Whoever sent this has been digging into MacKenna for a long time to have accumulated all this information. Can't help wondering who it is and why they're looking into Matthew and Owen." Destiny scrolled through another file, and glanced at Dane. "Maybe somebody wanting you to take over MacKenna-Duncan International?"

He shook his head. Why was it so hard for everybody to understand he didn't want the company? He didn't want the money. He wanted the truth.

And with these files, he might finally get it.

WELL, HE'D DONE what he could to set Dane on the right track. If his boss found out what he'd done, Brian would get reprimanded at best, and fired at worst. He didn't care one way or another. He'd decided a long time ago he'd watch over the Boudreaus the best he could because he owed them far more than he could ever repay.

Brian remembered Ms. Patti's face when he'd shown up after snatching Tina out from beneath the bad guy's nose. While his motives might have been questionable, his intentions were good, and he'd kept the woman alive. That had to count for something, and heaven knew he could use some good karmic points.

He'd been the last person anybody expected to walk through the front door at the Boudreau ranch. Even though he'd been one of the Boudreau kids for such a short time, and ended up having to leave the Big House, he still considered it the best part of his entire childhood. Douglas and Ms. Patti had shown him more love and acceptance, treating him as if he mattered, than he'd ever experienced in his rotten life. Whether they knew it or not, they'd been the main reason he'd turned his life around and gone to work for the good guys.

Reaching into his pocket, Brian pulled out his wallet and removed the folded and creased letter inside. It was the latest one he'd gotten from Ms. Patti. Ever since the night he'd helped rescue Tina—which wasn't hard since he'd been the one to snatch her in the first place—she'd written him faithfully. Once a week like clockwork, he received a letter from his unofficial mother, keeping him in the loop of what was going on with the Boudreaus. Making him feel like he belonged.

The one time the letter didn't show up on time, he'd practically accosted the mail carrier, demanding to know why it was delayed. And wouldn't that have gone over well with his superiors at the bureau. He could see the headlines now.

Undercover FBI agent assaults mail carrier, demands missing letter from home.

Home.

Funny how he thought about the Boudreau ranch as home. He'd lived there less than a year, and he'd been a holy terror the whole time. Yet no place before or since, gave him the same feeling of belonging as that ranch, and the family who owned it.

He'd spent the last few months investigating Matthew MacKenna, based on information the bureau gained from an informant, who'd ratted out the old man after he'd been caught with his hand in the proverbial cookie jar and summarily fired. When he'd been caught siphoning money from online accounts, he'd spilled his guts, trying to make a deal. The facts he presented hadn't made a whole lot of sense, not until you added all the pieces of the picture together. They were still missing a few key facts, but he'd figure it out. He always did.

Their information supplied details that seemed incredulous at first, because Matthew MacKenna was a seemingly upstanding businessman, ran a multibillion-dollar international conglomerate for decades without a whiff of scandal. At least on first perusal.

A cloud of suspicion hovered over MacKenna-Duncan International even two decades after the murder of Peter Duncan and his wife in a home robbery gone wrong and the disappearance of their kid. Brian was convinced Matthew MacKenna knew more about their deaths than what he told the police. Proving it was a whole different thing though.

The more he looked into Matthew MacKenna, the more he was convinced *he* hadn't been the one to pull the trigger that killed his partner. For one thing, he had an airtight alibi for the time in question. Could he have hired it out—bringing in somebody to do the dirty work? Absolutely. There were rumors that Matthew MacKenna didn't get his own hands dirty, but he wasn't opposed to having somebody else do the actual deed.

Exactly like his son did when he'd put out the contract on Dane Boudreau's life. Owen MacKenna was a chip off the old block, not hesitating to shell out big bucks to get the job done. The question nagging at him was whether it had been Owen's idea to hire a hitman, or whether he was doing Daddy's bidding.

When his boss at the FBI told him about the contract, Brian jumped at the chance to be the one they sent undercover. His reason was two-fold. The biggest reason—protecting Dane Boudreau. Reason number two—bringing down somebody who thought they could hurt the Boudreaus. Not going to happen on his watch.

Luckily, Brian specialized in undercover cases. A perfect example was his last big case, where he'd been hired to abduct Tina from Shiloh Springs. Fortunately, that turned out to have a happy ending. With some help from his buddies at the bureau, they'd contracted the mercenary site through a fictitious account and accepted the contract, blacklisting it for anybody else. Brian had been ordered not to contact any Boudreau to tell them about the investigation, and he hadn't—until he sent Dane the URL with all the information he'd managed to gather. Information currently sitting on an FBI server at Quantico.

Brian had one big question, though. Why was Dane investigating Matthew MacKenna? He knew all about the computer searches Dane had been running for years. The man had obtained copies of police reports, copies of statements from company employees. Dane probably knew more about the Peter and Marjorie Duncan case than anybody.

And now Destiny Smith was added to the mix. He smiled thinking about the quickie wedding he'd witnessed. He'd lied to Owen MacKenna when he'd stated he hadn't caught up with Dane in Vegas. Heck, he'd been on the same flight out of Houston they'd taken. Destiny had her own interesting past in California. She'd had her record expunged, but nothing was ever really gone, and he managed to find out all about Destiny's past. Fortunately, she'd turned her life around, coming out the other side a better person. And after watching Dane while they were in Vegas, he knew the man was head over heels in love with his new wife.

Hearing his text alert, he reached for his phone and got the message that the package had been delivered. Good. He'd done what he could to point Dane in the right direction. Now he had to hope Dane followed the bread-crumbs and got the information he needed.

While he did that, Brian needed to do his job—not the mercenary one he'd been hired for. Not the one the FBI thought he was working. Nope, he had one job and only one.

Keeping Dane Boudreau alive.

CHAPTER SIXTEEN

D ANE HAD LEFT about an hour earlier, going to talk to Dom, the ranch foreman who was covering for him while he'd taken time off to look into MacKenna. She'd grabbed a shower after he left, made some toast, and now sat at her laptop, ready to dig into the URL they'd received earlier. If the information contained at the ghost site was correct, they might actually be able to build a case.

Just not against Matthew MacKenna.

She heard the screen door creak open, followed by the front door, and swiveled in her chair to see who'd come in. It was a surprise to see Ms. Patti walk into the kitchen like she owned the place. Which in essence she did, since the house was part of the Boudreau ranch. Dane lived here and ran the day-to-day operation, but Momma Boudreau still pulled all the strings.

"Good morning, Ms. Patti. Can I get you some coffee?"

"I'd love some, but you stay where you're at. I can get it." Without hesitating, Ms. Patti crossed the kitchen and poured a cup, and then sat at the table across from Destiny. She hooked her huge bag over the back of the chair and folded her hands on the table.

Uh-oh. What did I do?

"I want to know what's going on with my son."

No beating around the bush for Ms. Patti. When she wanted to know something, she got right to the point. Destiny appreciated the trait.

"You know most of what's happened. We got information that's taking us in a different direction just this morning."

Ms. Patti shook her head. "That's not what I mean. I want to know what's going on between the two of you. I want to know how you feel about my son."

"I…" Destiny's voice froze. What could she tell Ms. Patti without disclosing the real reason she'd married Dane?

"Honey, I know I'm putting you on the spot, but y'all eloping blindsided his daddy and me. You barely know our son. I doubt you talked to him more than a time or two and then next thing we know, you're coming back from Las Vegas with a ring on your hand."

"Ms. Patti, I—we—it's complicated."

Ms. Patti shook her head and made a tutting sound. "Child, emotions are complicated. If caring for somebody, loving somebody, was easy, would it really be worth it?"

Somehow her words struck Destiny like a sledgehammer to the chest. Because she was right. Everything she felt for Dane came rushing forward, and tears prickled behind her eyelids.

"It wasn't supposed to be like this. Our marriage, it's a simple business decision. Whoever wants Dane dead might have second thoughts if they realize his claim to MacKenna-Duncan won't disappear if he dies. I've promised to continue the fight to get justice for his biological parents and protect their legacy." She drew in a ragged breath and twisted her hands in her lap. "I don't care about the money. I care about Dane."

"I know you do, honey. Every time you look at him, I can see how much you love him."

"You can?"

"Of course. A mother knows these things."

Destiny stood and walked to the counter, staring out the window above the sink. "I didn't realize it myself until we were in Vegas, and I got hit by the car. The only thing I could think about was Dane, and how much I loved him." She laughed. "I barely know him, and I can't believe how quickly my feelings went from being an acquaintance to being head over heels in love with him."

"Wait, wait. You were hit by a car?"

She gave Ms. Patti a shaky smile. "Long story. I'm fine, just a few bruises. Ms. Patti, what am I going to do? Our marriage isn't real. Dane doesn't feel anything for me, except maybe friendship. Maybe not even that. All this happened because I kept my eyes on everything related to your family. Like some obsessed stalker. Just saying it out loud, it sounds like I've got mental problems."

"Just tell me this one thing. Do you love my son enough to fight for him?"

"I've never felt like this before. Not about anybody. I love him with all my heart."

Ms. Patti rose and walked over, pulling Destiny into her arms, embracing her with a warmth of affection Destiny hadn't felt in years. Her own mother hadn't been overly affectionate, though Destiny knew she was loved. But this? The generous sharing of affection made her realize how much of life she'd allowed to pass her by.

"As long as you love him, everything will work out. I know Dane cares about you too."

Destiny took a step back and wiped ineffectively at her nose. Great, she was blubbering in front of her mother-in-law. She straightened when the words Ms. Patti had said sank in.

"Did Dane say anything to you? About how he feels about me?"

Great, I sound like a whiny baby, craving attention like a teenage groupie with her first crush.

Ms. Patti reached up and caught her chin with her hand, her touch gentle. "He hasn't said anything, but I'm his mother. I've seen the way he looks at you when he thinks nobody's watching. If he's not in love yet, he's not far from falling."

Destiny let out a shaky breath, her heart soaring at Ms. Patti's words. Was she right? Could Dane have real feelings for her? Care about her even half as much as she did him? Was there even a small chance he'd want to make this sham marriage into a real one?

"I think we understand each other. I have one final thing to say, and then we'll sit down and finish our coffee. And I brought a fresh coffee cake with me, it's in my bag." Ms. Patti took a step back, putting distance between them, and Destiny felt it like a chasm gaping beneath her feet.

"Say it."

"I'll support you, help you win over my son's heart. But, if you hurt him in any way, I'll make you wish you'd never heard the name Boudreau. Are we clear?"

"Crystal."

Ms. Patti's smile was a thing of beauty, lighting her face with a glow of warmth and love. "Excellent. Let's have some cake, shall we?"

Without another word, Destiny reached into the cabinet and took down two plates. Suddenly, she was starving.

DANE STRODE TOWARD the barn, determined to deal with whatever crisis Dom had called about and get back home. Meet him in the barn, he said. Dane hoped it wasn't anything serious because he wanted to get back to Destiny. They were getting close, so close he could practically taste the satisfaction. He'd been sure Matthew MacKenna had been the man responsible for killing his biological parents, yet additional information provided by the anonymous source contradicted all the evidence he'd gathered over the years.

Walking through the sliding doors, he stopped short when he spotted his father and Rafe leaning against the stalls. Great, they'd set up a familial ambush. He glanced around, half-expecting to see more of his brothers tucked into the nooks and crannies, ready to ambush him.

"Son."

"Morning, Dad."

His father indicated the stack of hay bales piled along the far wall. "Get comfortable, we need to talk."

With a shrug, Dane sat on one of the bales, knowing his father would get to the point when he was ready, and not a moment before. Rafe hadn't moved, and he wondered what his brother was there for. Guess he was about to find out.

"Don't look at me. I'm still mad at you for not telling me sooner."

"Bro, don't start. I did what I thought was right. I was protecting you," he swept his hand between his brother and his father, "all of you."

"Do I look like I need protecting? I'm older than you and definitely wiser because this stunt has stupid written all over it."

"Boys, let's get to the point."

"Fine." Rafe glared at Dane. "But we're gonna talk later.

Count on it."

"Sure thing, Sheriff," Dane mocked.

Douglas took a step toward Rafe. "If you can't stop goading your brother, you can leave."

"Sorry, Dad. I'll behave."

Douglas sat atop a hay bale and turned his attention to Dane. "Your momma is worried." Dane knew better than to interrupt his father. "It broke her heart when you ran off and got married."

"Dad, I never intended—"

"I know, son. I'm not talking about my feelings. But your momma has a tender heart, especially when it comes to you boys. I think she's worried you got married, rushed into things, without thinking about all the pros and cons. Course, her biggest concern is if you're in love with your wife."

Dane pulled back as if slapped. He'd never thought about his feelings for the beautiful woman he'd all but commandeered into a slapdash wedding. His reasoning was sound: he needed to protect his family's legacy, to make sure MacKenna couldn't take away everything his father had spent his life building. MacKenna had controlled the company, the finances, everything for over two decades, and he needed to make sure measures were taken to change that fact. Not for himself; he couldn't care less about the money. He was happiest on the back of a horse, riding the land. But the people who'd been there for his father, working for him, helping make the company into a multibillion-dollar industry, deserved to be rewarded. The rest could be donated to various charities where it could do the most good.

"Before you answer, think. Destiny's a good woman, and she doesn't deserve to be hurt when you've had your revenge."

"Dad, it's not about revenge. It's about justice."

"Is it? Seems to me, if you're looking for justice, you wouldn't have done everything in secret. You've got valuable resources at your fingertips." He gestured toward Rafe. "Your brother's the sheriff of Shiloh Springs. Antonio works for the FBI. Derrick Williamson is the special agent in charge of the Austin FBI office. Heath works for the DEA and has governmental contacts. Ridge runs a security service, which is in high demand for being able to not only protect people, but to uncover threats to his clients. Lucas, with his investigative skills, knows how to dig deep into a problem and uncover facts deeply hidden. And what about Shiloh? He's a private investigator. Instead of working with your family, you've spent years hiding in the shadows, digging for evidence to destroy MacKenna. That's not justice, son. It's revenge, plain and simple."

Dane sat straighter, stunned at his father's words. Was he right? All this time, he'd thought he was seeking justice for an untenable crime, willing to do the work the police hadn't. But hearing his father state his goal wasn't justice but revenge—

"I don't know anymore. What I believed weighed against

what I now know, everything's upside down and isn't making sense. I want to see the person who murdered my parents pay for what they did, but I won't do it at the cost of losing this family. You know I wouldn't change a single minute of my life here. I love you and Momma. I even love the big lug over there." He waved his hand in Rafe's direction.

"Right back at you, bro."

Douglas smiled and stood, placing his meaty hand on Dane's shoulder. "We love you, too, son. Now that we've straightened that out, what am I supposed to tell your momma?" Dane didn't understand what his father wanted him to say. "About Destiny. She wants to know if you're in love with her."

He didn't hesitate. "I love her with every fiber of my being. She found that empty place in my heart and filled it to overflowing. I hoped we'd have time after things are over for me to spend time with her. Let her know how I feel."

"Don't wait." Dane turned toward Rafe at his bold statement. "I almost lost Tessa because I was afraid to tell her how I felt. Thought it was too soon, we were moving too fast. Don't make the same mistake, because you'll regret it for the rest of your life. If you love Destiny, tell her. You might discover she loves you too."

"Thanks. I can't lose her. If it means giving up every-thing to keep her, I'll do it. I'll let go of chasing after MacKenna, give anything, if she'll stay with me. Love me half as much as I love her."

The truth of those words echoed in his head, and he realized the moment he admitted the truth, let go of all the anger, the burning rage at avenging his parents, the love for Destiny filled him, giving him peace.

"I think we're finished here, son. Go home and tell your wife how you feel. Finding the one woman in the world that's meant for you and only you, it's a special thing. One you don't want to miss out on because you weren't strong enough or smart enough to realize what you had until it's gone."

Dane pulled his father into an embrace, thanking God for leading him to the man who would teach him how to be truly worthy of Destiny's love. He'd led his sons by example, showing them with his words and his actions how to be the best father and husband any woman could ask for.

"Thank you for being my father."

Douglas gave a jerky nod and strode out of the barn, leaving Dane and Rafe inside.

"Dude, nice to see you finally realized what's truly important. I'm outta here. I'm having lunch with the woman I love. See ya."

Dane watched his brother leave, smiling. They might give each other grief from time to time, because that's what brothers did. But when the chips were down, they were there for each other—always.

He couldn't wait to get home, to the woman he loved.

He only hoped it wasn't too late to tell her how he felt, and that he was going to drop the investigation, and live a life filled with love. With her, if she'd stay with him.

There wasn't any other option.

CHAPTER SEVENTEEN

AFTER MS. PATTI left, Destiny changed clothes and headed toward town. She needed to stop by her apartment, and pick up a few things, especially since she was spending more time at Dane's place. A couple more changes of clothes would be nice, since she only had basically what she'd taken to Las Vegas with her, and she was getting tired of doing laundry.

Leaving a note on the table for Dane, she turned on her music, choosing her favorite list. The soft classical music played in the background, while her mind tried to sort through her earlier conversation with her mother-in-law.

Wow, it felt so strange to think about Ms. Patti as her mother-in-law. But once they'd gotten past their conversation about Dane, she'd treated her like one of the family—and it had felt nice.

When her phone rang, she hit the Bluetooth on her steering wheel without stopping to see who was calling, instantly regretting it when Owen MacKenna's voice came through the speakers.

"Good morning, Destiny. I trust you and Dane got

home okay."

"Owen. How'd you get my phone number?"

"It wasn't hard. A couple of quick calls, an assurance that I was your cousin, and wham, bam, instant access."

"Fine. What do you want?"

"Destiny, why all the hostility? I thought we had a lovely time at dinner."

She shook her head, knowing there had to be more behind his call than simple pleasantries. While they'd been civil, and their dinner cordial, there hadn't been anything implied about furthering their relationship. Besides, he'd known the whole time that she was with Dane, married to him, yet he hadn't said a word.

Of course, I wasn't forthcoming with him, either.

"I'm sorry. I'm in a lousy mood. What can I do for you, Owen?"

"I think we should talk. About Dane Boudreau."

"My husband." She put a deliberate emphasis on the word, making sure Owen had no doubt about where her loyalties lie. Something told her he was fishing for information, and she wasn't about to tell him anything. If he needed to know something, he should man up and ask Dane himself.

"Yes. Congratulations by the way."

"Thanks. I'm sorry to be abrupt, but I've got a lot of things to take care of this morning. Was there something you needed?"

"Actually, I believe it would be of benefit to us both to talk. I have some information regarding your husband you should know. Critical information which could change his life."

She shuddered at his words. Though his tone was pleasant, the words not giving away much, something about the way he said them sounded threatening.

"So, talk. What do I need to know about my husband?"

The pause that followed her words had her thinking they might have been disconnected, but she heard his sigh over the line. "This isn't something we can discuss over the phone. I'd suggest we meet face-to-face."

"Unfortunately, Owen, I'm no longer in Las Vegas, so that might be a bit difficult."

Ball's in your court.

At the sound of a horn, she looked up and waved as Brody drove past, heading toward the Big House. She hadn't seen much of him; he'd been spending all his time with Beth. Pregnant with his child, she'd had a health scare a couple of weeks ago, and the doctor had put her on bed rest. Maybe she'd check with Ms. Patti that afternoon, see if there was anything she could do to help.

"Actually, I'm in Texas. I had business in Dallas. If you're amenable to the idea, we could meet someplace. Trust me, the information I have to share with you is life-changing."

Thinking about everything Dane had endured, and all

the time and effort he'd put into getting justice for his biological parents, she knew she couldn't refuse. What if the information Owen held was the final clue to bringing down the man who'd killed Peter and Marjorie Duncan?

"Fine. How do you want to do this?"

"I'm actually on the road now, headed toward Shiloh Springs. I should be there in a couple of hours. How about once I hit town, I give you a call, and we can pick a place to meet?"

"Alright. I've got a couple of errands to run, so I'll be around town anyway. I need to go by my apartment and pick up some things. I'll expect your call."

"I look forward to seeing you again, Destiny."

He disconnected the phone call, and she couldn't help wondering what Owen was up to. Was he planning to share information about his father's role in the Duncan's deaths? Or did he want her to talk to Dane about stopping his investigation into his father's culpability? Whatever he wanted, she wasn't going to play go-between. If he wanted to give Dane information, he needed to speak with him. And she had no problem telling him exactly that.

It took another thirty minutes to get to her apartment after the call, and she pulled into her parking space, already going through the list of what she needed to get while she was there. Clothes were a must. She needed to pick up her other laptop too. Being able to have programs running on one while she worked on another was a habit she developed.

It kept things running at peak efficiency, and she rarely lost data, because she had consistent backups by having multiple systems.

Walking to her front door, she slid the key into the lock and opened it. She tossed her bag onto the hall table and headed for the kitchen to grab a bottle of water before she started packing.

She'd barely made it halfway before an eerie feeling crept over her. Something wasn't right. Turning in a slow circle, she studied the living room, the kitchen, and the hall leading to her bedroom and office. Nothing seemed overtly wrong, yet the uneasy feeling persisted. The tiny hairs on the back of her neck stood at attention, and if she didn't know better, she'd swear she wasn't alone. But nobody could be inside her apartment. The door had been locked, and nothing was out of place or missing.

Yet she couldn't shake the feeling. Moving on instinct, she slowly walked into the kitchen and pulled the largest knife out of the block on the counter.

I'm being ridiculous. Nobody's here.

Taking soft steps, she checked the living room, glancing into each corner. Nothing. Drawing a deeper breath, she opened the hall closet, pulling the door open fast, and taking a step back, the knife gripped in her hand tight enough it hurt.

Cautiously, she moved to the spare bedroom, the one she'd set up as office space. It was the one room in her apartment that was cluttered, because when she was working, she tended to shove things around. It was calculated chaos. Anything she wanted or needed, she could find it almost immediately, but anybody looking at the mess would think she was a slob.

She froze in the doorway, eyeing the scene. Something was off, like things had been rifled through. Whoever had been in her office tried to put things back, but they didn't have an understanding of her quirky filing system or the way she stacked thumb drives and equipment.

Somebody searched my office.

Seething outrage built, along with the feeling of being violated. How dare somebody invade her sacred space?

She backed into the hallway and glanced toward her bedroom door. It stood ajar a few inches—which didn't feel right. Normally she kept it closed, especially when she wasn't home. But she'd been rushing when Dane showed up to take them to the airport for their quick elopement to Vegas. Maybe she hadn't been paying enough attention and left it open?

Sliding her hand into her back pocket, she pulled her phone free and swiped her thumb across the screen. She pulled up her list of contacts, looking for Rafe's number. Maybe she was being paranoid, but better safe than sorry. If she called him out on a wild goose chase, she'd apologize, but she couldn't shake the feeling of dread deep in her gut. And she'd learned a long time ago to follow her gut, because when she didn't, bad things happened.

She pressed the call button and lifted the phone to her ear, heard the first ring. Before the second ring, a hand reached over her shoulder and the phone was snatched from her hand. Stark terror enveloped her, and she spun around—to face Owen MacKenna.

He tossed her phone on the floor, and stomped on it with his heel, crushing the screen and the case. The smile he shot her was triumphant and creepy. Wildness shone in his eyes, tinged with a side of crazy, and she knew she was in trouble.

"What are you doing?"

"Keeping you from making a stupid mistake. Can't have you calling Dane and having him come riding to the rescue like a white knight, can we?"

She started to slam her hands on her hips, but stopped, remembering the knife she still held in her hand. It was down by her side, and she wondered if Owen had spotted it. Shifting her weight onto the balls of her feet, she drew on her self-defense training, easing into a stance to give her the best momentum if she needed to defend herself or to go on the attack.

"I wasn't calling Dane. I was calling you. I figured we could meet at Daisy's Diner in town. It's on Main Street and it's easy to find and has great food. How did you get into my apartment? And for that matter, why are you in my apartment? I've gotta tell you, Owen, your actions aren't imbuing me with a lot of confidence. Matter of fact, you're scaring me."

"Destiny, you should be scared. I know all about what you and Dane have been up to with your computer searches. Looking into my father's records, digging into his life. All your digging and prying has him a nervous wreck."

She started to deny his accusations but thought about it for a moment. If he knew, there was no reason to hide what they were looking for. Get him talking, and maybe he'd reveal something important.

"It took me longer than it should have to figure out why Dane was looking into MacKenna-Duncan International, and specifically Peter and Marjorie Duncan and their connection with my father. We had no idea who Dane Boudreau was in the beginning. He was some yahoo in Podunk, Texas, who showed an inordinate amount of interest in my father and our company. I had the head of security check him out. Dane Boudreau was nobody. A man who'd been adopted into a family of nobodies. I wasn't worried. Not until I saw a picture of him." Owen shook his head and made a tutting sound. "He's the spitting image of his father. Mine almost had a heart attack when I showed him the photo. Thought Peter was back to haunt him."

Destiny had noted the uncanny resemblance between Dane and his biological father, though she'd never mentioned it. It was simply another piece of the puzzle to be fitted into its spot, to reveal the whole picture. Funny that it might be the thing that brought the whole mountain of conspiracy tumbling down around them.

"I'm going to ask again, Owen. Why are you here? Were we getting a little too close to uncovering the truth?"

"The truth?" His bark of laughter sent a chill across her skin, raising goosebumps. There was a tinge of madness to it, and she wondered if Owen had slipped over the edge. "I know all the so-called evidence you and Dane have collected. You may have good computer skills, but my guy is a genius. He installed software on Dane's computer that not only cloned his hard drive, but it tracked every keystroke, every website he visited. Dane didn't make a move that I didn't know about."

Ugh. She wanted to bang her head against the wall for being stupid. One of the first things she should have done when she started working with Dane was check his computer. But she'd allowed her personal feelings for him to cloud her better judgment, but she hadn't been on her game from the minute she'd met him. Now he was going to pay for her clumsiness. Some hacker she was. The lightbulb finally went off, and she realized they'd been wrong. So wrong. About everything.

"You're the one who executed the contract."

"You're finally catching on. One of my better decisions if I do say so. Putting a contract on your husband kept him scrambling, unfocused, and with his attention divided, he wasn't as much of a problem."

"Why now? Dane's been digging into MacKenna-Duncan for years. Were you afraid he'd find something incriminating? Did you have something to hide, Owen?"

Don't tip your hand. The more he talks, the more you might find out. As long as he's talking, he's not trying to hurt you.

"We didn't care how much digging a stranger did into the company. There's nothing to find. My father has kept anything to do with MacKenna-Duncan squeaky clean. Nothing underhanded. No corners cut. As far as we knew, Dane Boudreau was simply a man looking for dirt— something he wouldn't find. Until I saw his picture, and I knew who he really is." He slammed his fist against the wall, close to her head, and she jumped, shocked at his impulsive show of violence.

"He's Dane Boudreau. Son of Douglas and Patricia Boudreau. He's lived in Shiloh Springs most of his life."

"The key words being *most of his life*. Before he came to Texas, he lived in Denver with his parents."

"His parents?" She tried to imbue her question with a hint of surprise, like she didn't know what he was talking about. Keep him talking, and hope Dane found the note she left. The longer she was away from the ranch, the bigger the chance somebody might come looking for her.

Owen's voice got louder with frustration, and Destiny barely held back a wince. "Stop acting like you don't know what's going on, Destiny. You aren't stupid. You probably know as much as Dane, maybe more. Is that it? Are you in it for the money? Did you marry him, thinking you'll get a big windfall when Dane makes a play for the company?"

"I married Dane because I'm in love with him."

A mournful look crossed his face and then was gone, so quickly Destiny thought she'd been mistaken. He slowly shook his head, and reached into his waistband, pulling free a gun.

"Then I'm sorry. Because you're in too deep, know too much."

"Owen, wait. Let me talk to Dane. I can convince him to let things go. He'll stop digging, he won't go after your father for killing his parents. I can make him stop, but it'll never end if you kill me."

Owen looked at her, opened his mouth, and then closed it. He looked confused, like he hadn't understood what she'd said. What part had bamboozled him? While he hadn't mentioned Dane knowing the Duncans were his parents, it was a foregone conclusion. It had to be—

"He thinks my father killed his parents?" He raised his hand to the side of his head, the gun against his scalp. "That's wrong. My father didn't kill Peter or Marjorie." Lowering the pistol to point at her chest, his next words chilled her to her core.

"I did."

CHAPTER EIGHTEEN

D ANE'S PHONE RANG as he stepped onto the front porch of his house. After talking to his father, he'd wanted to race back home, pull Destiny into his arms, and tell her how he felt. Beg her to feel the same way he did, to love him. Instead, he'd stayed in the barn, brushing the horses, and taking stock of his thoughts. Knowing if he wanted to have any kind of life, he needed to let go of the burning hatred for Matthew MacKenna. To say goodbye to his biological parents, knowing they might never get the justice they deserved, and he had to be okay with that.

He called out to Destiny, but she didn't answer. Walking into the kitchen he spotted a piece of paper on the table. The note said she was headed to town to grab some things from her apartment and run a couple errands. She'd be back later. Her feminine handwriting brought a smile. The intimacy of having his wife leave a note for him made him chuckle. His wife. Guess it would take a while for him to get used to the thought.

Taking the steps two at a time, he climbed to the attic. He needed to box up everything he'd gathered about

MacKenna. The good, the bad, and the ugly. He'd give it to Antonio. Let the FBI decide if they wanted to pursue a formal investigation into the less-than-legal activities going on behind the scenes at MacKenna-Duncan. From this point on, he was done. He needed to get on with his life.

A life with Destiny, if she'd have him.

He pulled out his phone and took photos of the whiteboard and all the lists and facts written there. Thumb drives were tossed into a padded envelope. The external drive where he kept all his backed-up information joined the file folders in a box.

When the phone rang, he spotted Rafe's name on the ID. Since he'd just seen his brother less than an hour ago, what could he want?

"Did you forget something?"

"Is Destiny with you?" Rafe's question had Dane shooting to his feet.

"No, she's not. Why?"

"I got a weird call from her number. It rang once and then stopped. When I tried calling back, it's going straight to voicemail."

"That's weird. Let me check and I'll call you right back."

Dane disconnected and immediately dialed Destiny's number. Like Rafe said, it went straight to voicemail. The air felt squeezed out of his lungs when he tried a second time with the same results. Something was wrong. Destiny always answered her phone.

He immediately dialed Rafe back. "She's not answering me, either. Something's wrong. When I got back here, I found a note she'd headed into town to grab some stuff from her apartment and then had a few errands to run."

"Okay, let's not panic. Maybe her battery went dead or something. I'm at the sheriff's station. I'm going to head over to her apartment. I might be able to catch up with her there, and we'll find out it's nothing serious. Hang tight, I'll call you back as soon as I know something."

"Forget that, I'm heading for town. Go, see if you can find her. Call me if you find out anything."

"I figured you'd say that. Don't speed."

Dane disconnected, and raced down the stairs, grabbing his keys from the hook by the front door. Yanking it open, he stopped short at the sight of Brody standing on the porch, his hand raised to knock.

"Dude, what's the rush?"

"Destiny's missing."

Brody shook his head. "No, she's not. I saw her driving toward town, passed her on my way here. She appeared fine, though she looked like she was talking to somebody, might have been on a call."

Dane pushed past his brother, and jumped off the porch, making a beeline for his pickup, Brody running to catch up. Something deep inside, an instinctual primal urge, screamed something was wrong. Time was of the essence, and every minute he wasted away from her ratcheted up the tension coiled in his gut.

"Rafe just called, said he'd gotten a call from Destiny. It rang once and disconnected. He hasn't been able to get hold of her since. She's not answering my calls, either."

"Hold up, bro. I'll come with you."

He waited long enough for Brody to slide onto the seat. Revving the engine, Dane squealed out of the drive, tires flinging up dirt and gravel. He couldn't waste time. What if somebody had taken Destiny to get to him? They'd already tried to kill her with the hit and run in Las Vegas. The video footage showed it wasn't an accident. Had somebody hurt her in retaliation for his digging, his search for evidence against Matthew MacKenna?

"Killing us isn't going to help Destiny, bro. You need to focus, get a hold of your emotions, and shut them down. You can't go into this without thinking things through. What did Rafe say exactly?"

"He got a call from her number. It cut off abruptly after one ring. He called back but Destiny never answered. He's headed to her apartment."

Brody's hand gripped the overhead strap white-knuckled because Dane was doing over a hundred miles an hour. Nobody better get in his way, because he wasn't stopping or pulling over until he hit the town's limits.

"Why her apartment? Isn't she living with you now that you're married?"

"She still has a lot of stuff at the apartment. We haven't

had a chance to move everything. There was a note on the table when I got home, saying she was heading to town to pick up some clothes. Rafe's checking there first."

"Makes sense. Bet her battery died, and she hasn't noticed."

"Nope. If she was making a call and it cut off after one ring, she'd have plugged the phone in. All her equipment's still at her apartment; she'd have a phone charger. I feel it in my gut, something's wrong. What if somebody's taken her, to get back at me? I've made a lot of waves digging into my biological parents' deaths." He swallowed hard, past the lump lodged in the back of his throat. "I'll never forgive myself if she's hurt because of me."

"With everything going on with Beth and the baby, I haven't had a chance to ask if you're out of your ever-loving mind, keeping something like this from your family? You let us think you didn't remember anything about your life, kept the fact your biological parents were murdered, and you eloped with Destiny. Did I leave anything out?"

"Nope, think you covered the highlights. How is Beth doing? Everything okay with the baby?" He swerved around a car, passing him without slowing. Why was everyone driving like they were headed to Sunday church with a casserole on the backseat? He stepped harder on the accelerator, willing the old pickup to go faster.

"They're both fine. She's bored out of her head being on bedrest, but Momma and the other women are stopping by, keeping her company, dropping off meals, and keeping Jamie occupied." Brody shot him a glare. "Slow down. You won't help Destiny if you get us both killed."

"I have to get to her. I know something's wrong. It's like a voice screaming in the back of my head. She's in danger. She's hurt. I don't know what's happened, but it's not good." He slammed his hand against the steering wheel. "I can't lose her, Brody. She doesn't even know how much I love her. I married her for all the wrong reasons, but the right one, the most important one, is that she's my whole world. She brought a light into my life I hadn't known was missing. One look at her and I was gone."

"That's how it was with my Beth. I waited because she'd been through so much with her ex. Raising a little girl on her own, moving halfway across the country so she could be with Tessa. Wondering if wanting her might cause problems with Tessa and Rafe. In the end, none of that mattered. The only thing that does is love."

Dane slowed as he got closer to town, stomping down the urge to ignore everything except getting to Destiny. But he wouldn't endanger others. Adrenaline rode him, mixed with a healthy dose of fear.

I have to find her. Have to save her. Never let her go again.

Racing into the apartment building's parking lot, he screeched to a halt at the front doors, pulling behind Rafe's car. He didn't spot his brother anywhere. Jumping from the truck's cab, he heard Brody get out, and he ran for the doors, bursting through them. Not waiting for the elevator, he sprinted for the stairs, taking them three at a time. Brody matched him step for step, and within minutes they'd arrived on the third floor. Shoving open the stairwell door, he stopped when he spotted Rafe standing outside Destiny's apartment, his gun drawn.

Rafe raised a finger to his lips and jerked his head toward the front door, where a small opening was visible. Dane quietly made his way to his brother.

"The door was like this when I got here. I hear two voices in there. Destiny and Owen MacKenna. She mentioned his name, that's how I know it's him."

Dane reared back like he'd been slapped. "Owen? That doesn't make sense. What would he want with Destiny?"

"I can only hear bits and pieces, but it sounds like Destiny's trying to get Owen to talk. He really has a hard hatred on for you, bro."

Dane shook his head. "That can't be right. Owen hasn't seen me since he was a teenager. We used to play together. He'd have no reason to hate me."

"You're trying to put his father in prison. I'd say that's a good enough reason." Brody laid his hand on Dane's arm. "I know you want to bust in and rescue Destiny. Wait, see what he says. He might spill something you can use against his dad."

Dane shook off Brody's hand. "I don't care about that. That's what I was doing when Rafe called. Packing everything up. I'm done. I'll give it all to Antonio, and the FBI can decide if they want to go after Matthew. All I want is Destiny."

Owen's voice got louder and Rafe waved a hand at his brothers for quiet.

"Stop acting like you don't know what's going on, Destiny. You aren't stupid. You probably know as much as Dane, maybe more. Is that it? Are you in it for the money? Did you marry him, thinking you'll get a big windfall when Dane makes a play for the company?"

"I married Dane because I'm in love with him."

Her words slammed into Dane with the force of a sledgehammer. *She loves me?* It was his every dream coming true. Every Christmas, Easter, and birthday rolled into one, and still paled in comparison with the reality of Destiny loving him.

He needed to go to her, hold her. Tell her he loved her too. Brody grabbed his arm, pulling him back when he took a step toward the partially-open door.

"Stop. Listen." Brody's urgent whisper in his ear stayed him, as did Rafe's hand unclipping and pulling his gun.

"He thinks my father killed his parents?" Dane's blood ran cold at Owen's words. "That's wrong. My father didn't kill Peter or Marjorie. I did."

DESTINY'S GRIP ON the knife slipped at Owen's chilling words.

He killed Dane's parents? How is that possible? Everything pointed to Owen's father as the one responsible. How could we be so wrong?

"I don't understand, Owen. Your father killed Peter and Marjorie."

He scoffed, waving the gun wildly. "People are idiots. Sheep led around without a shepherd are easily misled. Plant a little misinformation here, a suspicious rumor there, and you can make people believe whatever you want."

Owen stood with his back toward the door. Destiny shifted her body around, trying to get her feet positioned for the most stability. If she needed to make a run for it, or stand and fight, she needed to rely on her training. Her hand tightened around the knife. She couldn't understand why Owen hadn't spotted it, but she was thankful for that small blessing, though knife versus gun wasn't the greatest odds.

From the corner of her eye, she spotted movement and fought to keep her expression blank. She recognized Rafe moving into her living room, slowly gaining ground with each step. She needed to keep Owen talking, distracted from what was happening behind him.

"Why, Owen? Dane said you were his friend. That you played with him when your parents had business meetings. He cared about you, said you were his buddy."

"I was his friend. He was a good kid. You don't get it. I

couldn't let Peter ruin my dad. I heard them talking; they didn't know I was on the patio outside Dad's office. Peter was going to break up the company. Everybody knew he was the brains, the one to come up with the new inventions, the next big thing. Dad was the money guy. He got their startup, invested everything we had."

"But the company was successful, right from the start."

I need to keep him talking. What he's saying, it's the first time I've heard Peter Duncan planned to sell. Not that I care. Please, Rafe, don't get caught. I can't have your blood on my hands.

"Exactly." Owen ran a hand over his face, sweat peppering his brow. "Within two years, MacKenna-Duncan was rolling in profits. Investors clamored to be part of our success. And Peter was going to toss it all out the window, and for what? Because he wanted to spend time with his family. He didn't care what his pulling out would do to the stock shares. A hit like that? It would take years, if ever, to rebound."

Rafe crept closer and she spotted the gun in his hand. She didn't want Owen to die, but she wanted to live. She wanted to tell Dane she loved him. There was still a gap in Owen's recounting, but they'd be able to fill in the blanks, she hoped.

She wasn't sure what alerted Owen to another's presence, but he grabbed her arm, and jerked her forward, wrapping his arm around her neck. The cold barrel of his gun pressed against her temple, and her breath caught in her throat. This couldn't be happening. Everything seemed to slow down, and for the first time, she understood the saying her life passed before her eyes. Because every moment she'd spent with Dane played in her head like a movie, brilliant color video clips. Them working together in Dane's attic, making notes and uncovering clues. Them sitting on the couch, watching movies, and eating popcorn. Their wedding in Vegas. Them kissing in the gazebo.

No. I will not die like this. Come on, girl, you've studied. You've practiced. Are you going to stand by like a wimp and let Owen blow your brains out, or are you going to fight back?

"Stop right there or I'll blow her brains out."

"Owen MacKenna, right? I'm Sheriff Rafe Boudreau."

Owen barked out a laugh. "Another Boudreau. Figures. You need to leave. This is between me and Destiny."

"And me." Dane stepped out from behind Rafe, and Destiny's knees weakened, threatening to buckle. How had she not seen him?

"Well, well. Wish I could say it's a pleasure to see you again, Thomas. Oh, wait, it's Dane now."

"Owen, it's over. I'm not coming after you or your father. I don't want the company, I never did. I wanted justice for my parents, but I don't care about that anymore. All I want is for you to let Destiny go. Take me in her place. Use me as a shield to get out of here. Rafe will let you go."

"Shut up, bro. MacKenna, don't listen to Dane, he's an

idiot. Let's talk, just you and me. We can make a deal, but you have to let Destiny go. You don't want to do this, man. There's nowhere for you to run. Let me make things easier for you. Put down the gun, and we'll all walk out of here. I give you my word, if you come with me now, it will be better for you."

"Don't you get it? It's too late. She," he tapped the gun barrel against her temple, "knows everything. I'll get the death penalty. Or some bleeding heart will give me life behind bars. You'd be better off shooting me now."

"Not gonna happen, Owen." Dane took a small step forward, his gaze shifting to Destiny, and she read in his eyes everything she needed to know. Nobody could fake that kind of love. She started to take a step and felt Owen's arm tighten around her throat, tight enough she couldn't breathe.

"Stop. I need to think."

"Owen, why'd you come after Destiny? She hasn't done anything to deserve your ire. She's innocent in all this. Please, let her go. I'll do whatever you want, give you anything. Don't hurt her. I'll beg if that's what it takes." Dane dropped to his knees, spreading his hands to the sides.

"Dane, no!"

She couldn't let him sacrifice himself. Without thinking, she raised the knife to the side and ducked, plunging the blade into Owen's thigh with all her strength. She felt it slide deep, felt the warm wetness on her hand as blood spurted from the injury. The gun tumbled to the ground when

Owen used both hands to grab his thigh, pulling the knife free and dropping it to the floor. Rafe rushed past her, kicking the fallen gun out of the way, and placing handcuffs on Owen.

Destiny ran and flung herself against Dane, tears spilling down her cheeks. She gave a hiccupping cry when his arms wrapped around her, squeezing her so tight she couldn't breathe. Heck, she didn't need to breathe.

"I love you," she heard him whisper against her hair. "I can't believe I almost lost you. Never, ever, scare me like that again. I almost lost you."

"You're never going to lose me, Dane. I love you so much."

Everything around her blurred, and she couldn't see anything but Dane's beautiful face, his eyes filled with love. She hoped he could tell how much she loved him, too.

Brody cleared his throat, and Destiny started to pull out of Dane's arms, but he wouldn't let her go. Not that she fought all that hard to get free. She was exactly where she wanted to be.

"Wrong place, wrong time for that, dude. Rafe's got to take Owen to get medical attention and then to jail, and you need to take Destiny over to see Doc Stevens and get her checked out. Rafe's going to have questions, but he wants her evaluated for shock."

Dane rose and held out his hand to Destiny. She placed hers in his, allowing him to pull her to her feet.

"How much did you hear?"

Dane rested his forehead against hers before answering. "More than enough to know Owen killed my parents. I think I secretly hoped I was wrong, and that maybe it had been a home invasion, and that Ginger panicked when she took me and ran. Knowing the truth hurts, but now it's out there."

"There are still more questions than answers at this point, but Owen's probably going to want to make a deal before he says anything else." Brody placed his hand on Dane's shoulder and gave Destiny a wink. "Don't give him a hard time about taking you to see Doc Stevens. He needs to know you're safe and unharmed. Trust me, the shock is going to hit, and when it does, you're going to need each other. Now, as for me, I'm going to offer to take a look at the knife wound in MacKenna's thigh, bandage him up and let Rafe take care of the rest. Them I'm going home and hugging my wife."

"It's over."

She nodded. "You have the answers you've always wanted. You'll have closure and justice for Peter and Marjorie." Leaning against his chest, she rested her head on his shoulder.

"Let's go home."

CHAPTER NINETEEN

A FTER HAVING DESTINY checked out by Doc Stevens, they ended up at the sheriff's office. Dane wanted to hear what else Owen had to say. Finding out that a sixteen-year-old Owen had killed his parents, deliberately gunned them down in cold blood was shocking. Unbelievable.

He opened the door to the sheriff's office and ushered Destiny in before him. Sally Anne was seated at her desk and glanced up when they walked in. She immediately stood and came over to him, wrapping him in a big hug, and then did the same to Destiny, whose eyes rounded with surprise. He smiled, knowing his gal would have to get used to it. Most folks in Shiloh Springs, once they got to know you, were caring and affectionate, and didn't have a problem expressing their feelings. Especially Sally Anne because she was considered part of the family, having worked with them for more years than he could count.

"Your brother's back in the conference room with the prisoner. There's also a couple of other people back there." She leaned in and whispered, "You're not going to believe who one of them is." Putting a finger to her lips, he knew she was dying to tell him, but had been ordered not to.

"Come on, sweetheart. Let's find out what's going on."

He made it about halfway down the hall when he recognized the voice speaking. Son of a gun, what was Brian doing here? He hadn't seen the man since the whole Tina and Chase kerfuffle, discovering that he'd been one of those his momma called her lost boys.

"I recognize that voice. This should be interesting."

Pushing open the conference room door, he spotted Rafe standing at the head of the table, his hands flat on the tabletop, leaning forward and talking to…Matthew MacKenna.

Wasn't that a surprise?

"Come in, Dane, Destiny. You're part of this and deserve to hear what Mr. MacKenna has to say."

"Dad, don't do this. I already confessed—"

"Son, not another word. No more cover ups, no more lies. Thomas, I mean Dane, you deserve to know what really happened. I've held onto the truth of that night for over twenty-five years. We didn't know you were alive. When you disappeared, I hired a PI company to look for you. They coordinated with the head of security at MacKenna-Duncan." Matthew MacKenna shook his head, shoulders slumped. He seemed to age before Dane's eyes, guilt and despair written on his face.

He pulled out a chair, and helped Destiny into it, before sinking onto the chair beside it. From the sound of things, they were going to be there for a while.

"Can we start from the beginning? Owen admitted to shooting my parents. Over money." Dane couldn't keep the anger in his words from boiling to the top. He hadn't wanted the money. Couldn't care less about it. He'd lived his entire life without the millions his biological parents had. Learned from the Boudreaus what was really important in life, and it didn't start or end with dollar signs.

"Don't blame my father. He didn't know what I planned. Not until it was too late." Owen leaned back in his chair and scrubbed his hands over his face. The shiny metallic handcuffs encircling his wrists sent a wave of satisfaction through Dane.

"If I had, maybe I could have stopped what happened. My best friend, his wife, gunned down because of a stupid mistake."

"What kind of mistake, Mr. MacKenna?" Rafe asked.

"Peter Duncan and I started MacKenna-Duncan. Right from the start, we knew we'd struck gold. The company flourished and grew to the point we couldn't keep up with its success. Peter was the brains. He could analyze and make anything. Give him two pieces of wire and a stick of chewing gum, and he could design something amazing. I couldn't match his skills or his desire to create. He was a bona fide genius. I had a different skill set. I knew people, had connections to money men. I'd always been called a born salesperson, and I became the money guy."

"So, what changed? Owen said my father wanted to sell the company. That he wanted to spend more time with his family." He slammed his fist onto the table, causing it to shake. "How was it wrong to want to enjoy a family life with his wife and son? There's no justifying killing a man because he loved them."

"What are you talking about? Peter didn't want to sell the company. We planned on opening two new branches, one in New York and one in London. Nobody was talking about selling."

"That's not right, Dad. I heard you talking. Peter said he was pulling everything out of the company, all his shares. It would have bankrupted us."

Matthew's eyes widened and he started choking. Destiny jumped from her chair and pounded him on the back. After a bout of coughing, he reached toward his son. "That wasn't what he said, Owen. Nobody was selling the company. We talked about setting aside a portion of the company for you. You and Thomas. We planned on transferring a block of stock into a trust for you both, to make sure you were taken care of financially for the rest of your lives."

Owen shook his head, vehemently denying his father's explanation. "That's not right! I know what I heard. You were yelling, shouting about everything falling apart if he sold. Don't lie."

Matthew closed his eyes, his expression pained. "We fought about selling a large block of shares, not the company. Peter wanted to diversify his portfolio, to invest in some risky stock. I told him he was making a mistake. We were still too new a company to pull in the old guard investors. He'd never have gotten what the shares were worth. I got Peter to agree to talk with our CFO, and get the trusts set up in a way that didn't endanger anybody outside the company picking up more shares than we could afford to sell."

"But…no…that's not right. He was going to sell the company. I know what I heard. He was going to steal away your future, our future. I couldn't let that happen."

Dane sat silent, watching the interaction between the two men he'd hated for so long, and felt nothing but pity. How many lives had been destroyed because of a teenager's mistake?

Matthew turned to face Dane, his expression pleading. "Owen called me in a panic after he'd killed your parents. He was crying, pleading with me for help. What was I supposed to do? He was sixteen years old."

"You helped him cover up what he'd done, didn't you? Somehow made it look like a home invasion gone wrong. He killed your best friend. Your business partner. He killed my mother. How do you justify murder?"

Destiny slid her hand into his, squeezing tight. He silently admitted he was glad to have her at his side. Without her there, he might have lost it, but he had to be strong for her. She'd endured enough for one day, coming so close to losing her life. It scared him, how he might have missed out on the best thing to ever happen to him. All because of a lie.

"He's my son. I couldn't let him go to prison. I immediately came when he called me. It was too late for either of them; they were gone. I searched for you, I swear. Combed the house from top to bottom, but you were gone. I really did search for you, Thomas—Dane—but never had a clue what happened to you."

"Tell me what you did, Mr. MacKenna," Rafe said. "We need to know everything. Did somebody help you tamper with the evidence to make it look like they were killed by a burglar? Forensically, it couldn't have been easy."

"Jerrold Greenspan, our head of security at the time, helped me. He was a former detective for the Denver Police Department. We hired him when the company got big enough to need a physical building and staff. I knew I could count on him. Peter never knew because he left all the hiring decisions to me, but Jerrold left the DPD under less-than-ideal circumstances. There were unsubstantiated rumors about his taking bribes from drug dealers and looking the other way for enough money. He could be manipulated for the right price and knew his way around contaminating any possible DNA evidence."

Dane leaned forward and stared at Matthew. "You're using the past tense when describing him. Is he dead?"

"Yes, heart attack, three years ago. I have to admit, I didn't mourn him or his constant demands for money to keep his mouth shut." MacKenna made a moue of distaste, and Dane marveled at the older man's inability to see his hypocrisy.

"You've hidden the truth for over twenty-five years." Rafe towered over Matthew, and he shrugged.

"Which one of you discovered Dane's real identity?" Destiny asked the question Dane wanted to ask, but he'd waited, wanting to hear what kind of excuse Matthew might give.

"That was me." Owen gave her a little wave from across the table, handcuffs encircling his wrists. "Because I'm a paranoid fool. I've always suspected Thomas was still alive, and he'd show up one day and tear everything down from the roots up. I've had a computer expert who's a pretty darn good hacker, keeping tabs on anybody accessing information on my dad or me. When Dane started digging, it set off an alert."

"And you immediately assumed it was Peter Duncan's missing son? Seems like a pretty big stretch."

"Sheriff, I said I was paranoid, not stupid. I had the PI come to Shiloh Springs and get DNA from your brother. Had it tested against Peter's. There's absolutely no doubt he's Thomas Elliot Duncan."

"I've heard enough." Dane rose and shoved his chair back hard enough it slammed into the wall. "Rafe, I don't care what happens with either of them. That part of my life is over. Let the Denver PD or the feds handle it."

Brian moved away from the wall and leaned his hip on

the edge of the big conference table. He'd remained silent the entire time Matthew and Owen had been revealing all the facts about his biological parents' deaths. So quiet, Dane had all but forgotten he was there.

"We're not finished, Dane. Still a few things you need to know before the MacKennas get turned over to pay for their crimes."

"Why are you here, exactly? You're turning into the proverbial bad penny, showing up in the middle of the action. Don't tell me, you're smack dab in the middle of this, too?"

Destiny leaned closer and whispered, "Who is he?"

"Sorry, sweetheart, I forgot you hadn't met him. His name's Brian, and a long time ago, he was one of the lost boys who lived at the Big House." He saw the surprise on her face and could almost see the wheels in her head turning, working out what that entailed. Though she'd never met him, he'd bet his momma had talked about the FBI agent who'd kidnapped Chase's fiancée, Tina, in a convoluted scheme to keep her from being killed.

"Ms. Smith, nice to meet you. Congratulations on your marriage. The ceremony was lovely."

Dane shot him a glare. "You were there?"

Brian smirked. "I'm just glad I didn't see you in your underwear."

Dane heard Rafe's choked back laugh and shot him an I'll-tell-you-later look.

"I've got a buddy at work who owes me a favor. He lets me know whenever there's any suspicious activity associated with certain names."

Destiny punched Dane in the arm. "See, I'm not the only one who's checking up on you." She turned to Brian, shooting him a smile. "You saw the notice about the contract on his life, didn't you?"

"Yes, ma'am. I got the go-ahead from my bosses to accept the contract, and get it blacklisted, so nobody else could accept it. Somebody less scrupulous, who'd have no problem putting a bullet between your husband's eyes."

"Are you the one who took a potshot at me?"

Brian scowled. "No. Somebody shot at you? When did that happen?"

"About two weeks before Destiny told me about the contract. If it wasn't you, it must've been somebody being where they didn't belong. Happens sometimes. Usually a hunter straying onto land where they shouldn't be."

Rafe dragged a hand through his hair. "Anybody else feel like they've fallen down the rabbit hole? Brian, when you say your bosses gave the okay, you're talking about the FBI?"

"What? He's a fed?" Owen's head fell forward to rest against the table. "I hired a fed, thinking he was an assassin? Might as well throw me under the jail now because I'm dead meat."

"People, people. Let's focus. Brian, you talk. Everybody else, shut up." Destiny waved a hand toward Brian, as if she hadn't just told him to continue. Dane noted the twinkle in the other man's eyes and realized why his momma liked him so much. He vaguely remembered Brian, but he'd been young enough and still too scared that the rug would be pulled out from under his new life to pay much attention, and before he knew it Brian was gone. Too bad he hadn't been able to stick around the Big House longer when he'd been a kid. He'd have fit right in with his brothers.

"Yes, ma'am. I've worked undercover in similar cases. You want more details, you can talk to your husband or Rafe. But this case was personal, so I took a keen interest in keeping Dane alive. I've tracked his every move, while coordinating the mercenary contract with MacKenna Junior here." He reached over and popped Owen in the back of his head.

"Hey!"

"I fed Junior just enough info for him to think I was doing the job. I have to admit, I was surprised to find out they wanted you dead because of your real identity. Don't be surprised when the feds come around, because there's going to be a lot of people going down in this case. Not to mention the SEC and a bunch of other agencies with alphabet names." And you," Brian pointed at Dane, "you were looking in the wrong place, chasing the wrong person."

Dane stared at the other man, realizing he'd been played by an expert. "You're the one who sent the note. The one with the URL that pointed me onto a different course."

"Now you're getting the whole picture, bud. By the way, lose that URL. You never saw it. Delete it from your computers." He shot a glance toward Destiny, and she nodded.

Rafe straightened from where he'd leaned against the wall during Brian's recitation. "I think we're about done here. Everybody will have to make official statements, so be prepared to come back. Owen, Matthew, you've both been read your rights, but I'd strongly suggest you talk with your lawyers. Yes, I know you waived your rights at the beginning of this interview, but in light of the disclosures made, I'm advising you to reconsider. Brian, do your bosses need a copy of the video of this interview?"

"Definitely."

"Alright, anybody who's not a MacKenna, go home. I've got a ton of work to do."

"Excellent." Brian headed for the door. "Think I'll check in with your mother while I'm in town." Shooting Dane a jaunty salute and winking at Destiny, he strode out.

Dane stood and offered his hand to Destiny. "Sweetheart, let's go home. We've got a lot of talking to do."

"We do, but only one thing matters. Tell me again that you love me. Nothing else matters. We'll get through anything together, as long as there's love."

CHAPTER TWENTY
EPILOGUE

Two days later

"WHAT HAPPENS NOW?"

The family had gathered at the Big House. Two days had passed since Matthew and Owen MacKenna were arrested. The FBI showed up before Rafe even got their statements and paperwork done, taking both into federal custody. He'd seemed happy not to have to deal with the national press descending like a swarm of locusts. Father and son immediately got transferred to Denver to get the whole mess sorted out.

Liam moved outside while the rest of the family stayed in the house. Dane and Destiny finally accepted the way they felt, relieving a lot of worry off his shoulders. Over the last few years, Liam had watched his brother throw himself into running the ranch, building the herd with selective breeding, excellent feed, and care into one of the premier cattle ranches in the state, probably in the whole south. But in doing that, he'd sacrificed any kind of personal life.

Until Destiny barreled into his life intent on keeping

him from getting his head blown off.

The feds made sure Dane knew he'd have to come to Denver, not only to re-establish his identity as Thomas Elliot Duncan, but once all the smoke cleared, he had some serious decisions to make regarding MacKenna-Duncan International. A logistical and financial nightmare in the making, one Liam knew Dane dreaded. He didn't want the money, considering it cursed.

He leaned back on the loveseat and propped his feet on the coffee table. Stretching his arms out on either side of the back cushion, he grinned. Momma would have a conniption if she saw him with his feet on the table. But she wasn't here now, and what she didn't know wouldn't get him slapped upside the head.

"Your sister said I might find you out here."

Liam grimaced at the sound of Brian's voice. The guy had shown up earlier, invited by his parents. Something about him rubbed Liam the wrong way. Might be because he remembered Brian from the time he'd spent at the Big House. He'd been surly, unappreciative, and downright mean spirited most of the time. Of course, people change over the years, but Brian straddled the line of right and wrong, existing in shades of gray.

"Needed a few minutes of peace and quiet. It gets a bit stifling with so many people crowded around."

Brian lowered onto one of the chairs across from Liam, and matched his posture, propping his feet on the tabletop.

His dark eyes studied him, and he scratched at the short beard shadowing his face. Liam had to admit, the man looked tired. From what Brian explained, he'd been working behind the scenes ever since he'd discovered somebody was out to kill Dane.

"Can I ask you something?"

"Shoot. I'll answer if I can."

"What's your interest in my family? I remember you, from when you were here. You hated every minute you were 'forced to live in a children's prison.' Made Momma and Dad's lives a nightmare. Yet every time I turn around, you've got your nose up in our business."

Brian took his feet off the table and leaned forward, resting his elbows on his knees, hands hanging loosely between them. His posture screamed he was about to reveal a confidence, earnest and meeting his gaze directly.

"I'd think you'd be thankful I've kept my eyes on the Boudreaus. If I hadn't, your family would be looking at two deaths, maybe more. I remember you too." He gave a sarcastic laugh. "Always following me around like you didn't trust me. Were you afraid I was going to steal the family silver? Good call, because back then I probably would have."

"You tried to act like this tough guy, a chip on your shoulder so big you could barely carry it around. Too bad you had no clue how good you had it."

"Hindsight and all that, dude. I got older and I got wiser. Went through enough to realize what I'd tossed away. You have no idea how lucky you are. Douglas and Ms. Patti, they are rare souls indeed. My job shows me the snake pits out there, where people are a commodity to be bought and sold—especially kids. If there's a dollar to be made, nobody cares about the ones that fall through the cracks."

Liam felt the truth of Brian's words to the depths of his soul. He'd seen firsthand how despicable people could be. There wasn't a day that passed that he didn't thank his lucky stars he'd been placed with the Boudreaus. He'd been given a family, a life, and hope, a commodity he'd lost for a very long time.

"I know exactly how fortunate I am. I'm a Boudreau by choice—theirs and mine. But you still didn't answer my question."

Brian chuckled and ticked an imaginary one with his index finger. "Once I got hauled back by CPS, I had my eyes opened. Not going into details, but let's just say it wasn't happy, fun times. Made me wish every night when I closed my eyes that I was back here. Doing chores, getting three meals a day. Having Ms. Patti drop by my room every night, making sure I knew she cared. Long story short, when I got to a place where I could check up, see if things were okay with Douglas and Ms. Patti, I did. It became a habit after a while, watching the family. Seeing their businesses grow and prosper. Each one of the boys they'd brought into their family grew into strong, responsible men. Ones they could be proud of. Don't think I missed the little detail of the name changes when y'all were old enough."

"A tradition Rafe started. He was the first one Momma and Dad brought into their home. They weren't allowed to legally adopt him; his biological father wouldn't allow it. As soon as he was able, he petitioned to become a Boudreau. Each one of us that wasn't legally adopted has done it. Our tribute to the amazing people who've given us more than we can ever repay."

"See that's it. That's the thing I missed because I was a snot-nosed idiot. If I had it to do all over again…" Brian's words trailed off, but Liam got it. "With my job, I'm in a unique position to do things, have access to information regular law enforcement wouldn't. There's somebody in my office, an IT genius, who owes me more than one favor. He keeps tabs on everybody related to Douglas and Ms. Patti. That includes all their children, even you."

"Waste of time, man. I work construction. Not like I'm going to get in trouble there. Dad's company does everything above board. Honest. No cutting corners, no cheating on bids."

Brian's nod told Liam that he'd already known that information. Good. He didn't need to be on anybody's radar. He didn't have any secrets. It was easier to tell the truth than keep straight all the lies that spiraled out of control when you lied.

"I know. Anyway, I've got something for you." Brian pulled an envelope out of his pocket, folded and creased, like he'd had it for a while. "What you do with this, well, that's your business. A lot of time has passed, feelings change. But I figured you deserved to know the truth."

He tossed the envelope onto the loveseat beside Liam and stood. "Your momma has my number. Call me if you want to know more." Without another word, he turned and walked back into the Big House.

Picking up the envelope, Liam tapped it against his hand. From the stiffness inside, he knew it contained a photograph. Something about the contents of this envelope had his insides cramping, and his hands sweating. Stupid reaction to something that appeared innocent and unimportant.

He slid his finger beneath the flap, and reached inside, pulling out the single black-and-white photo. A woman stood silhouetted beneath a large oak tree, her blonde hair cascading over her shoulders, her head thrown back. She was laughing and smiling at the camera. Her eyes twinkled with suppressed mirth. They were blue, a startling almost sapphire color. He knew because the memory of them was indelibly etched in his memory.

Ruby. Beautiful Ruby, the woman he'd loved with every fiber of his being. The woman who'd captured his heart and his soul, giving his life purpose.

Ruby. The woman who'd died in his arms.

He held back his scream of rage and flipped over the picture. Written on the back were two words. Words he'd never thought to read.

She's alive.

Thank you for reading Dane, Book #10 in the Texas Boudreau Brotherhood series. I hope you enjoyed Dane and Destiny's story. I loved writing their book. Dane's the calm, even-tempered brother, the rancher who's been hiding secrets from Douglas and Ms. Patti for years. Now those secrets are about to come full circle, and somebody will stop at nothing to make sure they stay hidden. Even if that means killing Dane Boudreau.

Since so many readers wrote, asking about some of the secondary characters in Shiloh Springs, I decided some of them deserved to have their own stories told, and allow them to get their *happily ever after*. This doesn't mean you won't be getting the rest of the Texas Boudreau brothers, it simply means you're getting additional books about the folks living in Shiloh Springs and their interactions with the family.

The next book up is Liam Boudreau. Liam handles the day-to-day workings of the Boudreau Construction Company with his father, Douglas. Liam lost the one woman he loved years ago, and he's kept his heart closed off ever since. But his tidy world comes crashing down when he's blindsided with unbelievable news. Two little words on the back of a photo change his life completely. Want to know more? Keep reading for an excerpt from his book, Liam, Book #11 in the Texas Boudreau Brotherhood. Available at all major e-book and print book stores. Available for pre-order now.

PRE-ORDER LINKS TO BUY LIAM:
www.kathyivan.com/Liam.html

LIAM

LIAM RAN HIS fingertip across the face in the worn photograph for the hundredth time since Brian handed it to him days earlier. The guy seemed to turn up like a bad penny every time a threat to a Boudreau reared its ugly head. He'd helped uncover the truth about the hit on Dane's life. He'd even kidnapped Tina, Chance's fiancée, to keep her safe.

But the biggest bombshell he'd dropped as far as Liam was concerned? Giving him false hope. It was cruel, a punch-to-the-gut blow that turned his world on its head. Every time he looked at the smiling face in the photograph, the brilliant blue eyes of the woman so happy and vibrant, his gut knotted. The grief he'd held close for so many years weighed him down like a boulder atop his shoulders. The desolation and loss he endured—still did—threatened to consume him until nothing remained but a husk of what he'd been. It would hardly differ from what he was now, because he'd been little more than a zombie moving through life since he'd lost her.

He turned over the photo and read the two words print-ed on the back. Words that shook him to his foundation.

She's alive.

It was impossible. He'd been there when the paramedics worked on her, struggled to keep her breathing. Keep her heart beating. Followed the ambulance to the hospital, watched as the gurney swept past him into the emergency room.

Heard the long wail as the heart monitor flatlined.

He'd buried her along with his heart that cold, dreary Friday afternoon and hadn't truly felt alive a day since. Now, with two seemingly insignificant words, his entire world shifted on its axis.

Brian had taken off before he got a chance to demand answers, disappearing like a phantom in the mist. He really hated the guy.

"Hey, boss, you got a minute? Harry's got some ques-tions about the layout and he needs you to sign off before the guys start."

"Be right there."

Liam slid the picture inside his wallet and into his pock-et. He didn't have time to deal with ghosts from the past. He had a job to get done, and a crew to supervise. Boudreau Construction might be his dad's baby, but Liam had worked there for years, gaining the trust and respect of all the members of his crews. Now, he was second in command only to his father, who was giving Liam more responsibility and easing his way closer to turning over the reins of the company. It wouldn't be soon, but he felt a sense of pride and accomplishment when he looked at what he'd helped build.

After dealing with the questions about the condos' revised layout and changes to the blueprints, he pulled out his phone and dialed his mother's number. None of his brothers seemed to have a way to contact Brian, another fact that was driving Liam insane. How could the man keep showing up, disrupting their lives, and then going along his merry way without leaving a phone number or an e-mail? He knew his momma had Brian's number; he'd stated as much the last time Liam had seen the man. Which had been right before he'd tossed the envelope containing Ruby's photo into his lap and left town.

"Good morning, honey. Tell me you made your dad grab something to eat this morning. He snuck away before breakfast."

Liam chuckled at his mother's concern. Trust her, always making sure everybody was okay.

"Hi, Momma. Yes, we stopped and picked up breakfast sandwiches, juice, and coffee from Daisy's on the way to the site. He's full and in the trailer working on paperwork."

"Which means he's in a grumpy mood. He'd much rather be out working with the crew, getting his hands dirty. Anyway, what can I do for you?"

Liam heard the hum of the engine, the barely there music playing on the radio. Momma must be on the way to one of her listings. He didn't worry about her showing properties. She managed one of the prestigious real estate companies in Central Texas. At least not much. Patricia Boudreau was far too trusting, and he worried some unscrupulous idiot might try to take advantage of her. Then he remembered his mother had ten able-bodied sons and one take-no-prisoners husband, and the worry faded.

"Do you have a way of contacting Brian? Phone number maybe?"

"Why?" He heard the underlying edge of caution in her voice.

"Don't worry, Momma, he's not in trouble." *Yet.* "I need to clarify something he mentioned when he was here."

"You sure? Because you've been on edge for the last couple of days. Don't deny it. I'm your mother and I notice everything. Especially when my son's pulling himself back, distancing himself from the rest of the family. I promised your dad I'd stay out of it, give you a chance to come to us. But if you're looking for Brian…"

He couldn't do it. He couldn't open her heart to the same ache he'd gone through the past few days. Ruby had been like a daughter to her. Watching his momma grieve all over again when the truth came out? It would never be worth it. Besides, until he had proof, it was all speculation. Smoke and mirrors meant to disorient and befuddle the mind. Too bad it was working.

Could he let it go? The not knowing, the constant niggling in the back of his head wonder if Ruby was alive. Was somebody playing an enormous cosmic joke on him, just to watch him go insane? Even if it opened him up for untold misery, he had to know the truth.

"Momma, don't worry. You know what, never mind. I don't need to talk to Brian. It's not important."

"Liam Boudreau, who do you think you're talking to? You might lie to yourself, but you can't get away with lying to me. Tell me what's wrong, because if you don't, I'm going to call Brian myself and find out what's going on. And you know I'll do it."

Liam sighed, because he knew he'd just opened a whole new set of problems. There wouldn't be any keeping momma out of things now. If he didn't head her off, she'd pull in Dad and all his brothers, which was the last thing he needed to happen. He'd tell them eventually, because if Ruby was alive somewhere and needed him, he'd do whatever it took to find her, bring her back home.

(Book #11 Texas Boudreau Brotherhood series) © Kathy Ivan

PRE-ORDER LINKS TO BUY LIAM:
www.kathyivan.com/Liam.html

NEWSLETTER SIGN UP

Don't want to miss out on any new books, contests, and free stuff? Sign up to get my newsletter. I promise not to spam you, and only send out notifications/e-mails whenever there's a new release or contest/giveaway. Follow the link and join today!

http://eepurl.com/baqdRX

REVIEWS ARE IMPORTANT!

People are always asking how they can help spread the word about my books. One of the best ways to do that is by word of mouth. Tell your friends about the books and recommend them. Share them on Goodreads. If you find a book or series or author you love – talk about it. Everybody loves to find out about new books and new-to-them authors, especially if somebody they know has read the book and loved it.

The next best thing is to write a review. Writing a review for a book does not have to be long or detailed. It can be as simple as saying "I loved the book."

I hope you enjoyed reading Dane, Texas Boudreau Brotherhood Book #10.

If you liked the story, I hope you'll consider leaving a review for the book at the vendor where you purchased it and at Goodreads and BookBub. Reviews are the best way to spread the word to others looking for good books. It truly helps.

BOOKS BY KATHY IVAN

www.kathyivan.com/books.html

TEXAS BOUDREAU BROTHERHOOD
Rafe

Antonio

Brody

Ridge

Lucas

Heath

Shiloh

Chance

Derrick

Dane

Liam (coming soon)

Brian (coming soon)

NEW ORLEANS CONNECTION SERIES
Desperate Choices

Connor's Gamble

Relentless Pursuit

Ultimate Betrayal

Keeping Secrets

Sex, Lies and Apple Pies

Deadly Justice

Wicked Obsession

Hidden Agenda

Spies Like Us

Fatal Intentions

New Orleans Connection Series Box Set: Books 1-3

New Orleans Connection Series Box Set: Books 4-7

CAJUN CONNECTION SERIES

Saving Sarah

Saving Savannah

Saving Stephanie

Guarding Gabi

LOVIN' LAS VEGAS SERIES

It Happened In Vegas

Crazy Vegas Love

Marriage, Vegas Style

A Virgin In Vegas

Vegas, Baby!

Yours For The Holidays

Match Made In Vegas

One Night In Vegas

Last Chance In Vegas

Lovin' Las Vegas (box set books 1-3)

OTHER BOOKS BY KATHY IVAN

Second Chances (Destiny's Desire Book #1)

ABOUT THE AUTHOR

USA TODAY Bestselling author Kathy Ivan spent most of her life with her nose between the pages of a book. It didn't matter if the book was a paranormal romance, romantic suspense, action and adventure thrillers, sweet & spicy, or a sexy novella. Kathy turned her obsession with reading into the next logical step, writing.

Her books transport you to the sultry splendor of the French Quarter in New Orleans in her award-winning romantic suspense, or to Las Vegas in her contemporary romantic comedies. Kathy's new romantic suspense series features, Texas Boudreau Brotherhood, features alpha heroes in small town Texas. Gotta love those cowboys!

Kathy tells stories people can't get enough of; reuniting old loves, betrayal of trust, finding kidnapped children, psychics and sometimes even a ghost or two. But one thing they all have in common – love and a happily ever after). More about Kathy and her books can be found at

WEBSITE: www.kathyivan.com

Follow Kathy on Facebook at facebook.com/kathyivanauthor

Follow Kathy on Twitter at twitter.com/@kathyivan

Follow Kathy at BookBub
bookbub.com/profile/kathy-ivan

Made in the USA
Monee, IL
11 December 2021